Mark of the Maker

Sharon K. Angelici

DEDICATION

For my husband, my daughter and my so[illegible] [yo]u inspire me. I'm grateful for the minutes, days, and [illegible] with you, living this adventure called life.

For my Aussie family, including our rescued greyhound fur babies. We get through all of this, together.

For my parents, thank you for making adventure a real part of my childhood, and for encouraging me to become exactly who I was meant to be.

For the magic makers at Write with Light, thank you for all of your support.

For Hill, the late-night messages, and notes in the margins make stories and songs come together. Thanks for all of them.

CHAPTER I

Recovery

I was six years old the first time they caught me running wild through the woods. My feet were calloused and bare, and it was one of the few times I remember feeling like I belonged. I recall with great clarity the waving finger after, but there was no real punishment. Social services removed me from that home a week later. No one cared.

Wisdom at six was a survival instinct. It came from a place I didn't understand, but when I was quiet and very still, something I couldn't define was always pulling me in the right direction. I saw adventure everywhere, but in reality, mine was a world I wanted to escape. When it came to the whispering calls of the earth, I would discover that I had the wisdom of a thousand crones.

They called me Wildwood, although I didn't know why. Before I could read, I'd learned to find serenity in the howl of the wind. As a child in foster care, I lived with the uncertainty of an adult world shuffling me to unchosen places.

Putting my hands to the earth reminded me that touching it, letting it fall between my fingers, I'd always understand where I belonged.

I, the adult Wildwood Blackstone, barely existed on paper when I turned eighteen. I believed I didn't matter to anyone. That's how I felt aging out of the system. There was no safety net. I didn't have choices like most, but I loved working with my hands.

I always believed my origin story was a horrible cliché. In reality, there was no actual record of my birth, and by the time I'd entered the home where the woman I called Gran lived, that became the first chapter of my past. I had been a child without an ancestor, but not without a place to grow.

"I am who I am." It was my mantra, thanks to the only woman I ever called mother, Mama Pierce. It came from years of questions without answers and reconciling that the unknown would not be an obstacle for my future. It couldn't be, because all I knew was foster care and the endless track of people who'd been chosen at random to act as my family.

Here I stood at twenty-eight, waiting for my permanent blacksmith shop, earning the grant from the small town of Bannock. They welcomed me, not only for what I created but for what I promised to do. When I walked into the office of the town hall receptionist, she looked up from her work. "You must be Ms. Blackstone?"

I put out a hand to her. "Wildwood. Please call me Wildwood."

"Of course. Wildwood, welcome to Bannock. You must be excited to move into the building?"

I nodded. "I am. I guess you've got some papers for me to sign and a key?"

"Yes, I do, dear." She walked across the office and opened a cabinet door. She carried a thick folder and the rustiest skeleton key I'd ever seen. "These are all the historical documents I have about the building. There's a welcome note from me, and here is the key to the castle." Her smile was comforting.

"My castle. I like the sound of that." I picked up the folder. There was a form attached. "Should I sign this card?"

"Right by the *X*, and the building is all yours." I took a deep breath and held it in as I scribbled my name on the line. I was the owner. I had something to care for and call mine.

It was hard to believe my luck as I drove the few blocks through town. The carriage house wasn't much to look at from my curbside view. The combination of fieldstone and aging barnwood made it feel like a trip through time. I could imagine the original builder scavenging the rocks from the unclaimed farmland and milling the lumber by hand. When I closed my eyes, this is how I imagined an authentic blacksmith shop would appear. It was rustic, and I was ready to take on the challenge, confident that I could restore the structure to its original glory.

As I stood in front of the door, it appeared they were taking advantage of me, but I was confident the project would be the adventure of my life. I could also identify with the history of this cold, empty space. Being abandoned didn't make it useless. I understood that from my own journey. With a little patience and a lot of hard work, I would turn this long-vacant building into something beautiful.

I unpacked my car, looking down at my supplies and equipment, which amounted to a few duffle bags, some salvaged tools, and the welder gifted to me by Earl. Meeting that generous old guy was a gift.

"I'm here about the sign in the window. Are you still looking for help?" I asked the man behind the cash register.

"It's for repair and assembly. Do you have any experience with that?"

"A little." I wasn't lying. I knew how to use tools. Plus, how hard could it be to put a bike together?

"You ever had a full-time job?" He opened up a folder on the counter and pulled out an application.

I shook my head. "No, sir." The truth was that I was never in any place long enough to have one.

He handed the paper to me. "Fill this out, and bring it back. We can talk then."

I took it from his hand, eager to get started. I sat in the beat-up Volkswagen I called home, taking my time to answer all of his questions as best I could. I wrote the word car as the answer for address, worrying that he might use it as a reason not to hire me. It was the truth. It took me less than fifteen minutes to fill out the entire form and return to the store counter.

The man looked up at me. "That was fast."

"I really need a job, sir."

"Wildwood Blackstone." He read through the form. "You're living in your car?"

"It's a long story," I explained.

He interrupted. "You don't have any emergency contacts listed?"

"I was in foster care all of my life. I don't have any family, sir."

"Earl. Call me, Earl."

"I don't have any family, Earl. It's just me, and I live in that old bug out there." I pointed at the multicolored Volkswagen parked in front of his shop. "I really need a job.

"You can start at minimum wage, but I won't have you out on the street."

"I can't afford an apartment yet." I didn't know how to explain that the vehicle was better than a cardboard box.

"I'll let you live in the basement downstairs. It's not much, and you'll have to use the sink for cleaning up. We can try it out for a week and see how you work. That sound good?"

"It sounds really good, sir—I mean Earl."

"Bring your car around back, and I'll unlock the door for you."

It felt like an incredible moment of luck as I drove around the building and parked in the employee's only space. Earl was waiting for me.

"Bring in your stuff," he said.

I was too embarrassed for him to see that most of my belongings were the clothes I was wearing. "I'm good for now."

"Suit yourself. Let me show you the place."

The tour of the repair shop was quick, and I followed him to the living space underground. "There's not much for a bed, just that old cot. Do what you need to make it feel like home. No drugs, and no boys overnight."

I thought about both of his stipulations, remembering a childhood promise never to give up. "That won't be a problem."

He put a key in my hand. "This is yours for now." He left me standing in the middle of the room.

"Thank you."

"Don't thank me yet. You gotta prove yourself too."

"I will."

"You start at eleven tomorrow. Just come up, and I'll show you what you'll be doing."

"Okay,"

Earl had plans for me from the moment I walked into that bike shop on the following day. His faith in me was a gift. I wanted the carriage house to have the same setup I'd used working for Earl, but my modest equipment would have to work for now.

My cell phone buzzed in my pocket. I looked at the caller ID. "Hey, Jackson. How far away are you?"

"We're getting closer. Are you ready for us?"

"I sure am. I've been looking at these blueprints every day since they sent them to me. I think I rolled them out to sketch an idea each time I stopped for gas on my drive here. You're going to love what I've got planned."

I ended the call and threw my cellphone on the table. The air in the massive workshop felt cold and stale. I lit a bundle of sage and hoped the smoke would change the energy in the room. "Okay, mother Earth, give me some love." I sat down and put my hands to the ground. I could feel the spirit of this old building and realized construction wasn't the only work I needed to do inside.

Twenty-four hours later, Jackson, Mick, Vin, and Jamie rolled up in a road-weary van. I was finishing repairs to the sliding door of my carriage house when their voices startled me.

"Blackstone!"

These mismatched humans were my crew. "You made it."

"Finally." Jackson jumped out. His curly hair was a mess, and the rest of him matched a two-day road trip with three other people. "Vin took a little detour."

Jamie laughed as they opened the passenger door. "Little— fifty miles on a one-way forestry service-road is not little." Strong arms came around me for a tight hug.

"No railings and a sheer drop. I had it all under control." Vin explained. She exited the driver's side of the van and pushed Jamie aside to hug me.

"Where's Mick?" I asked.

They pointed to the back of the van. "Where do you think?"

"Sleeping," I said and laughed as I peeked inside of the vehicle.

"I don't think he was awake even when it was his turn to drive," Jamie said. They bumped the side of the car to wake the massive man. "Mick-o."

"That sounds about right," I said. "Let me show you where you can put your stuff. I hope you came ready to work?"

Mick jumped out of the van. "I'm ready." His arms came around my waist. "Show me what you got." He squeezed, picking me up off the ground.

"I've got hammers, saws, and a ton of work for all of us."

"Damn, girl, give us a minute." Jamie grabbed their gear from the back of the van.

"I'll give you five, and then we build."

They worked harder than I imagined. Day one was a frenzy of sorting, to determine what was salvageable construction material. I picked up a stack of old barn wood scrap we were planning to use upstairs. When I moved most of the trash away to reveal a broken patch of concrete and gravel, I felt the air around me shift. I couldn't explain it, but I wondered.

"That's weird," Jackson said.

"You feel it?" I was surprised that he sensed what I had.

"Feel, no. I just meant that big mess of the busted floor." He pointed at the patch of busted rock I'd just uncovered. "That's not going to be easy to fix."

"Oh, yea." I should have known he didn't feel the shift of energy. Only a few people in my life ever had, and being a foster kid brought a lot of people into my life. I looked at the fading scar in the palm of my hand. "She probably would have felt it," I whispered to myself.

"What'd you say?" Jackson asked.

"Just . . . nothing. I'll just add it to the list. And I did. Jackson stayed pretty close to me as we continued to work. He had a lot of questions and tried to make time for the two of us to be alone together. I had one thought in mind, and it wasn't him.

"What the hell was that?" I asked. The sound of shattered glass and swearing interrupted our conversation.

"It was Vin." Mick pointed at her.

"Shit— damn. I'm sorry, Wildwood."

The five of us stood outside the glass structure of the hidden rooftop greenhouse. I rolled the door closed to look at the broken window outside. I walked over to take a closer look, and waved my hand through the now-empty frame. The glass crunched under my feet. "I can't believe you aren't bleeding."

"It's weird. Maybe the glass is just brittle."

"Maybe, I don't know."

"I guess we should add that to the list?" Jackson was quick to start sweeping the mess.

"I'm not too worried. The glass won't even take a day to repair. I just have to order a piece." I took the dustpan and emptied it in the trash. That was the only crisis during the entire week. The days were long, and I admit I didn't give my friends any downtime. I was worried if they wandered far from the carriage house that I'd never get them to come back. Our last day together was the toughest.

"This place is shaping up." Mick and Vin were carrying the oversized clawfoot tub into the space of the bathroom. It was the last task I needed their help to accomplish.

"So that's it then?" Jamie asked.

"I don't know how to thank you all," I said as I walked to the kitchen. "It's hard to believe it only took a week to make the carriage house safe enough for me to live here."

Jamie laughed. "You know, you didn't let us do anything else, Blackstone."

"But look at what we built." I threw my arms out and turned around in the unfinished kitchen and living room.

Jackson laughed. "This is a great place for one person or maybe two."

"Is that a hint?" Vin shoved Jackson toward the stairs.

"Maybe, I don't know." He looked at me for an answer.

"I have other thoughts on my mind." I picked up the bedroll and oversized duffle bag. "I can't keep messing around with the four of you and get my business going." They followed me down the stairs and out to the parking lot.

"You've had a couple calls for repair jobs."

"I have, and that means I need to get focused and open the shop."

"So it's really time to go?" Jackson asked as we watched the others load the van. "You're sure you don't need me to stay longer?"

I knew what he was asking. "I'm sure. I have to do this for myself." He wanted us to be more, but that wasn't what I wanted . . . *he* wasn't what I wanted. "We are never going to be together, Jackson. I just don't feel that way about you."

"I know, but I had to ask."

"Thanks for being here and for helping me."

He leaned in for a hug. "I'm going to miss you."

I didn't know what else to say. He was a sweet guy, but I wasn't attracted to him enough to ask him to stay. "Goodbye, Jackson."

"Goodbye, Wildwood." He climbed into the back of the van.

"You're a real heartbreaker." Vin bumped my shoulder before hugging me. Jamie joined in just before massive arms circled the three of us.

"I love you, Blackstone." Mick set us on the ground.

"I love you too, big man."

Vin jumped in the driver's seat. "Don't be a stranger." She started the engine, gave it a rev, and they were gone.

CHAPTER II

A Pact

I stared out the oversized carriage house door, watching the van disappear. When it was gone, I spun around to look at the big empty workspace. I was finally alone, but I didn't feel lonely at all.

I sat down in the middle of the room and closed my eyes. I visualized my life in this space. I set my palms to the ground and felt the energy of the earth mingling with something I still couldn't define. I thought it might be a ghostly presence I'd heard about while researching the history of this town. Word on the street was that Bannock had spirits, and I was wondering if there might be a few inside my carriage house. I decided the best way to settle my curiosity was to get the blacksmith shop set up and running.

It began with a clean sweep of a worn-out corn broom. Remembering the woman I called Gran, I chuckled as the bristles gathered piles of dirt, rock, and dust. She had taught me to sweep, which was a big deal for a six-year-old. She had given me the chore, and I treasured the guidance and tenderness she passed to me, but I would always feel like the strange dark-haired girl who was as untamable as her name. I spoke to the silence of the room, "Oh Gran, I wish you could see this." It's funny how there were messages in moments.

Today marked my official second week inside the carriage house, and the longer I cleaned the open workshop space, the more uncomfortable I felt. The tiny vent windows were closed, and the doors latched tight, but there was a presence I just couldn't explain. I experienced light touches to my shoulder that were more than the brush of a breeze. It was clear that I wasn't alone, but there was no one I could see.

"Whoever you are, I'm armed. Please go away. Just leave." I took a slow, deep breath and reached to my side. The knife was where I kept it, loose in the deep pocket of my work pants. I pulled it out, and with the flex of my thumb and forefinger, flicked it open. I grabbed my phone from the other pocket and started to dial. "I want you to know I'm calling the police."

The dispatcher answered. "Nine-one-one. What's your emergency?"

"Hi, this is Wildwood Blackstone. I'm the new owner of the old carriage house on Fifth and Center. I'm not sure if someone is pranking me here or if it's just me, but is it possible for you to send an officer over to help me out?"

"Ms. Blackstone, are you in immediate danger?"

I stepped out of the center of the room until my back was against the door. "I'm not sure." I could hear the dispatcher calling for a car to respond. "I'm standing near the south exit of my building. Could you just send someone to help me out?"

"I've got units responding. Please stay on the line."

The two minutes between the response of the dispatcher and the heavy knock on the door seemed to pass in slow motion. My heart was pounding so hard, I could feel it in my head. I was startled by the different sounds. The knocking of the officer drowned out the voice of the dispatcher. "Police Department. Open the door, please."

"I'm going to hang up. Your officers are outside." I flipped the rusty latch on the handle and swung it open after stuffing the knife back in my pocket.

"Police, ma'am. Please step outside for a minute." I listened to the officer's command. "Please stand by my vehicle while I do a sweep of the building." Before I could take a step, I saw the flash of uniforms as three additional officers came through the open door.

Less than ten minutes passed from the moment they arrived until they searched the entire carriage house. I had time to question my feelings and second guess the decision to call for help. Had I been too hasty in making it? I was tangled up in my inner debate when the last officers of the search team exited the building. I saw the flash of red hair before turning to look into familiar beautiful green eyes.

"Wildwood," she said my name in a whisper. The smile on her face stopped me cold.

"Shay?" I wasn't sure what to do as she stepped toward me. Her arms came around my body. Our hug was quick, but the shock of seeing her again threw me off balance, and suddenly I was fifteen.

"What are you doing, Wildwood?" Shay yelled as her feet kicked through the tall grass.

I was lying on my back, hiding from the rest of the world. "Working." My naked feet wiggled deep into the dirt.

Her voice was a welcome distraction. "Doing what?"

"Listening." My eyes were closed, and my jet-black hair spread tangled in the grass, but hearing Shay's voice was the sound of love and friendship.

The sticks and leaves on the ground crackled and snapped as she stepped closer. "To who?" she asked.

I threw my arm across my face. "To what." I smiled, keeping my eyes closed to the sunlight, but I knew she would be confused.

"To who?" she asked again.

I grabbed a handful of the earth beneath me. "What." I held it, stretching above the tall grass.

She stomped her foot. "Wildwood, who are you listening to?"

I sat up, revealing myself so I could look at her. "It's not a who, Shay. It's a what." I turned my hand over, dumping the ground from my palm.

"Oh." She shrugged. "What are you listening to?"

I patted the patch of dirt beside me. "I'm listening to the vibrations of the earth." I waved for her to come closer.

"What does that even mean?" She twirled her finger beside her ear. "I mean, it sounds a little nuts."

I looked up at Shay, the red hair streaming across the skinny girl's pale face. "It's kinda hard to explain, and the truth is, I'm not sure you'll believe me if I tell you. "

She shrugged her shoulders. "Why don't you give it a try?"

I patted the ground, inviting her to sit beside me. "Okay, but you'll have to close your eyes." My fingers came up to touch Shay's face, and the tips drifted across the lids of her eyes. "What do you hear?" My hand lingered.

She took a deep frustrated breath. "I don't hear anything, really."

I reached to the ground and snapped a twig. "You hear that?"

Her eyes popped open, and she pushed at my leg. "Duh, yes . . . You broke a stick."

"Okay, now be as quiet as you can, close your eyes again, and really listen." Behind us, a flock of birds was singing in a tree, and in front of us, crickets chirped and squeaked a curious conversation. Through the tall grass, near the pond, frogs were singing to each other. We narrowed focus on the sounds of nature. "Now, what do you hear?"

Shay's nose wrinkled as she concentrated on each one. "I heard birds and some bugs and stuff, I think."

"Yes!"

Shay opened her eyes and crossed her arms, protesting my attempt to explain. "So you're listening to the animals? Why didn't you just say that, and what's it got to do with the earth?"

I shook my head. "It's not just the animals, Shay."

"What else is there?"

I threw my arms up, waiving them with wide untamed spirals. "Everything!" I grabbed her hand. "Come with me." We ran together through the tall grass to the edge of the trees surrounding the farm. We dropped to the ground, and I placed both of Shay's hands to the earth. The press was firm, indicating that I wanted her to keep them in this position. "Close your eyes and tell me, what do you feel?"

She thought for a long moment. "I feel gravel and sand, maybe some sticks and grass."

I smiled. "Well, yes, those are the obvious things." I placed my hands on top of hers. "This is going to feel funny at first." A warm energy moved through her hands and mine as we pressed harder to the ground. "Did you just feel that?" The muscles in her arms flexed, and she sat very still. Maybe it was shock or just curiosity, but her palm arched closer to the soil, staying under my own. She nodded. "That's what I hear when I'm listening, Shay." We sat still for a heartbeat. "Are your eyes closed?"

"Yes. I'm kinda scared to open my eyes right now."

I threw my head back, tossing my untamed hair off of my face. I closed my eyes tighter to focus, drawing the energy the ground gave me. I whispered, "If you become very quiet on the inside, the earth has a heartbeat just like our own. It's slow, but it's beautiful." We were face to face, hands on top of hands pressed firm to the ground. As if to call us together, the voice came from the wind.

"Just listen."

We lost track of time in the silence. Shay kept her eyes closed. I wasn't sure if she sensed the pulsing of the earth as I did, or if she felt my warm hands touching her own. I closed my own eyes, settled in a way I couldn't define.

"Wildwood?"

I was content to stay with her forever. "Yes."

Her forehead bumped against my own. "I feel kinda funny, and really tingly."

My eyes popped wide, and I saw Shay's pale face. "Open your eyes, Shay." I grabbed her shoulders. "Look at me." I gave her a gentle shake and waited as her green eyes fluttered open. She was always pale and fragile to look at, but at this moment, her skin was white as winter snow. "Lie down, Shay."

She fell against me. "I don't feel so good, Wil."

I was young, but I'd connected with the Earth's energy for as long as I could remember. I knew how to feel it, let it flow and not to hold onto it. I never considered that Shay would absorb it all. I pushed the red hair away from her face. "I know. I'm sorry." I wiped the sweat from her forehead with the sleeve of my shirt. "I'm so stupid. I don't know what I was thinking."

Green eyes fluttered as she tried to sit up. "You do this all the time?"

I nodded, holding and rocking her against the heartbeat pounding in my chest.

"Wow, Wil. It feels so . . . I don't know how to say it or explain it."

I pulled her tight against my body and held her close. The position was hardly comfortable, but it was comforting. I spoke across the top of her head. "So you're not freaked out?"

Shay shook her head as she wrapped her arms around me. "I'm really curious about so many things, Wildwood. Most of all, I'm trying to figure out how we've been in the same house for six months and you've never told me anything about this."

I leaned away to see her reaction. "Are you serious?"

She nodded and relaxed in my arms. We held each other in silence until she responded to my question. "I really am. Whatever just happened, it felt really good."

I squeezed her again before letting her go. I wanted to look into her eyes. "Promise you won't freak out?"

Shay dragged a finger twice over her chest. "Cross my heart. I promise. Please tell me."

"When I was about six, I was living in a different foster home. I was sitting on the front porch with Gran. We all called her that even though none of us were actually related to her. She was the coolest lady and I always felt lucky to be with her."

Shay nodded. She understood what it was like to be in a home that felt safe, even if it didn't last. I continued. "So one day, we were sitting together outside. Gran was only ever in the house to eat and to sleep. She was telling me a story about the plants in her garden. I closed my eyes because the sound of her voice was so perfect. She started to talk about summer rain and how important it was to nourish the world around us. I'm not one hundred percent sure what happened next, but I just felt the earth. It's like . . . it was just talking to me."

Shay interrupted, moving against my body, getting more comfortable in my arms. "What did it say?" She noticed the braided string around my wrist and rolled it between her fingertips.

"It wasn't words, really; it was a vibration, but I understood what it meant. It's kinda like how you keep up with Spanish. I understand earth."

"So what you just did here, how you made the energy move into us, you do that all the time?" Our fingers tangled together as we held hands.

"Well that first day, Gran explained it to me. She called it light work. It's like I know a part of me can be bright for someone lost, that what I do makes the earth stronger and makes people stronger. It's bigger than me. That's the way it is."

Shay traced the lines of my palm. "What we just did, have you done that with anyone else before?"

I shook my head. "Not like that. I've never really trusted anyone to understand." I rested my chin on her shoulder.

Shay stopped her gentle movements. "I trust you, Wil. I really do." We sat in the shade of an old tree, enjoying the heat of summer for a long time, neither wanting to let the other go. Shay was the first to break the silence. "So this light work . . . Can you teach me how to do it?"

I smiled. "If you really want to. I'm guessing most people don't feel what we just did."

"Where do we start?"

I closed my eyes, thinking of a way to make this special for her. "Sit up for a second." I wiggled my hand in my pocket and pulled out a tiny folding knife.

"What's that for?"

"Before we do anything, we have to make an oath."

"An oath for what?"

"We need to promise that no matter where we go or who we become that we will remember how all of this felt, and we won't give up on being whoever we want to be."

"Okay, yes." She wriggled back into my arms, adjusting until her left hand rested in my own. "Do it."

"Take a breath, and then let it out. Go really slow." She followed my direction, and, on her exhale, I scraped the tiny blade across what Gran called the Jupiter Mount. She didn't flinch as I mirrored the

small cut on my own palm. Shay turned and looked into my eyes as our palms clamped together. "You're a part of me, and I'm a part of you."

"Does this make us sisters?"

"It makes us so much more than that."

I had no way of knowing how accurate the vow was. Robert Frost once wrote, "Nothing gold can stay," and when it came to foster care, he was right. Shay and I lived in the same place for less than a year.

The memory of us in the tall country grass, our hands pressed to the earth, was a sudden blow to the balance of my world. "Holy shit! What are you doing here?"

She leaned away from the hug, but our hands stayed together. "Me? Bannock is where I landed a few years after they moved me from Mama Pierce's. Small town cop and all of that. What about you?"

I looked up at the building. "This is mine. I guess I'm the new scaredy-cat owner of the old carriage house."

"That's great. Amazing, really." Shay looked down at our joined hands. She noticed my tattoos at the same moment I felt the scars on her palms, and we let go. She adjusted the brim of her hat. "Damn, Wildwood. I guess I wasn't prepared to see you."

"I'm feeling the same. Today is such a weird day."

I watched her body language change from the teenager I loved back into the cop I didn't know. "So tell me what's going on. When Alex and I walked through the building, the second floor was empty. It looks like you've got a good start up there, though. You should get some boards on that broken window." She pointed to the first-story roofline. "If someone's coming in, it might be through there. I'll ask the third shift patrol to make a few passes tonight to watch the building until it's fixed."

My heart was racing, and the sounds coming from the big empty building spooked me, but the last person I expected to see was the girl who consumed my teenage dreams. "I've got a bunch of scraps piled up in the shop. I'll have it fixed by tomorrow. What I really need to know is how you ended up here in this small town, and of all things a cop."

Seeing her smile was a dream come to life. "There's a story behind all of that." She looked at her watch. "I don't have time to tell it right now. I need to get back and write a report, but I'm off duty in a few hours. How about I swing by and help you get that window squared away."

"I'd like that. I'll be here."

"Great." She tucked her notebook in her pocket and adjusted the radio clipped to her shoulder.

"Yeah, great." I raised my hand, giving an awkward half-wave. "I'll see you later."

I spent the rest of the afternoon sweeping and scooping the trash from the room. I thought twice about every dark corner and second-guessed the cold shifts in the air.

I cut scrap lumber to build a frame for the second-floor window. I piled the trash to make room for the saw. "Sorry to evict you, whatever you are," I was lost in thought when the cellphone in my pocket buzzed. "Hello?"

"Is this Wildwood?"

The voice on the other end was a surprise. "Shay?"

"Yes, it's me. I'm just finishing up for the day, and I thought I might stop by. You busy?"

"I'm building a frame for the window. I'll be working for a while." In a crowd, the size of my smile would have been embarrassing.

"Care to have some comp—?"

I responded before she finished asking. "I'd love it."

"I'll see you in a few, Wil."

It had been a very long time since anyone called me by that name. I held the phone to my ear long after it went silent. I dropped it back in my pocket. "Where have you been all these years, Shay?" I whispered the question to myself. I checked my watch every ten minutes, and by the time she arrived, I'd secured the window to the frame of the wall. The panes of glass slid into place, and my caulk beads created a seal that would keep out the rain. I was finished, standing on the roof, lowering my tools to the ground on a rope.

"You made quick work out of that." The voice traveled up from the sidewalk.

"I've got to be efficient when I'm on my own dime." I leaned over the top of the ladder. "I know I'm new to this little town, but when you said a few, I thought you meant minutes, not hours."

Shay was still wearing her hat, but she raised her hand to block the sunlight. "I decided to change just in case you were going to put me to work."

"That's too bad. That uniform looks so good on you." My bucket hit the ground, and I turned around and hopped down the ladder, two rungs at a time. "So . . . Officer Shay Cortland?" I leaned in for a hug.

She held on longer than I expected, but I didn't mind at all. "It's not Cortland anymore."

Thoughts scrolled through my mind, but the first was the reason behind the change and if it involved a long-term commitment. I wished I'd looked at the name tag on the uniform. "Officer . . .?"

"Pierce. It's Pierce."

I couldn't contain my smile. "You took Mama's last name?" I hugged her again, relieved that the change didn't involve a ring or a long white dress. My sigh of relief was louder than I'd intended, and when we separated, the smile on her face was a reflection of my own.

"After I turned eighteen, I wanted a new start. I never knew the Cortlands. I don't even know why that was my name. So I asked Mama if it was okay, and she said yes."

"Did you make her cry?" I knew the answer before I asked it.

"All the way to the courthouse and back." She shoved her hands in her pockets.

"She was wonderful." Our nod was simultaneous. "I had hoped I'd see you at her funeral. I was pretty wrecked."

Shay touched my cheek. "I was eight weeks into the police academy. I wasn't able to leave." My skin was warm beneath her hand. "I knew she was sick, but I never thought she'd be gone before I graduated."

"I looked through her notebooks and papers. She never told me anything about where you moved to or if you ever talked. I didn't know how to find you, but I was looking for Shay Cortland."

"I'm sorry I wasn't there for you . . ." She hugged me, and her hat fell to the ground. She picked it up, and in the same moment, wiped the tear from the corner of her eye. Her red hair fell across her face, reinforcing that she was still the most beautiful person I'd ever seen. She shoved the hat in her back pocket, running her fingers through her tangled hair. "I hope you can forgive me."

I watched her subtle gestures. The way she moved was different, confident, stronger. Her body had grown from the skinny, underfed, fragile teenager to a powerful, capable woman. "I knew there was a reason for your absence, Shay. I trusted. I've always trusted."

She took a deep breath and forced it through her lips. "That got heavy, whoa."

"Mama would have loved that uniform. She'd be so proud of you."

"She was the reason I joined the academy when I did. I was so scared, and she told me . . ."

"You are who you are," we said in unison.

I didn't hide how happy the memory made me feel. "Mama saved me."

"I'm pretty sure she saved us both." Shay bumped my shoulder with her own. "How about a grand tour?"

I liked the playful side of Shay. "Didn't you get the lay of the land earlier?" I pulled the cord of the extension ladder, and it dropped to the ground. For most of my professional life, I'd worked alone, and I was very efficient, balancing the ladder on one shoulder and carrying the bucket of tools in my other hand.

Shay watched with curiosity. "I was working. I didn't even notice you until we finished the search." She reached to take the tool bucket from my hand. "Let me help?"

"I've got it. It's balanced. Just grab the door." I dropped the supplies on the floor just inside the shop. "This is going to be my workshop." I waved my arms in the air. "I've got my oxy setup going here. That's a welding torch, and the forge will be permanent over there, after I pour some concrete. Before I moved I traded two blades for that grinder." I pointed at the tall table covered with an old bedsheet.

Shay interrupted. "Alex made me check under there." She read the confusion on my face, continuing to explain. "Alex was best friends with Reggie Benton, my field training officer a few years back. After the academy, once I was out on regular patrol, Al showed me the ropes. I called him a chicken shit for sending the woman half his size to check under the mystery tarp." She laughed. "A grinder, huh. I wasn't sure what the hell it was, but I knew it wasn't a threat."

I pulled the knife from my pocket. "I use it to finish these." This particular folding knife was the first I'd ever forged and was also my favorite. The blade was an experiment that turned out to be a profitable adventure.

Without warning, Shay stepped away. I had no idea that knives put her on edge. Her academy training taught self-defense against many weapons, but she also had a history that I couldn't have known. "Sorry, it's a reflex."

"Part of the job, I guess?"

"Something like that." She tugged at her sleeves and put out her hand to receive the folding knife. I noticed the scars again, but until she brought it up, I'd avoid the conversation. She wasn't ready to share, and I wasn't prepared to chase her away by asking too many questions. The blade was custom made, hand-forged with one-of-a-kind burled handle. "This is beautiful. You made it?"

It was impossible to hide my pride. "I started forging knives after I went to a blacksmithing workshop. I went to Dillion Tech for my welding certifications, and after I saw this guy work, all I could think about was making knives and blacksmithing." I took the knife from her hand. "This is called a friction fold." I opened and closed the blade, using both hands. "It's pretty basic, but it was tricky to make the first one. I split the wood for the handle more times than I can count, but I finally got it."

Shay tilted her head toward the blanketed grinder. "And that thing's for . . .?"

I lifted my backpack from the floor and tossed it on the old hollow-core door propped up on top of two sawhorses. The makeshift table was the perfect place to spread out my tools and work materials. I took out a sketch pad, opened it to the back, and ripped out a single page. In a quick second my knife blade flipped from the handle, and I drew it down the paper's edge. The slice feathered across without hesitation. "That grinder makes the rough finish shine and slice like it's going through butter."

Shay kept her distance even though I could see she was impressed. "That's a tiny bit intimidating."

"Nah. What good is a knife if it's not sharp?"

She shrugged. "Makes sense, and you use it as a giant honing stone?"

"More or less. The grinder gets me from rough forged to that mirror finish." I pretended to check my hair in the reflection on the blade. It was ridiculous since it was tied back and held in place by my cap.

She picked up the mask from the table and put her face inside to look through the dark green glass. "You're a welder?"

"I guess I am by profession. I built bikes in this cool little shop right out of high school. My boss, Earl, helped pay for my welding certifications. That's what I went to school for, but I do carpentry, and I've picked up a few skills along the way." I pointed toward the forge and all of the tools I had for blacksmithing.

"That sounds like fun." She set the mask on the table. "I'd love to watch you work sometime."

"I'd love to show you, but be warned—blacksmithing is kinda like a drug." I was fascinated by the way she handled the tools and materials on the table. "One try, and you might get hooked."

The sound of her laughter made me happy. "I'll risk it." She opened the spiral-bound sketchbook and flipped through the pages inside. "Are these projects?"

I nodded and stopped her from turning another page. "I have all of these ideas." I dragged my finger around the outside edge, tracing the picture of a hanging rack for the kitchen pans. "I just don't have the time or the scrap metal to make them."

"You just moved in." She closed the book. "If you're as driven as you were when we were kids, I'm sure you'll be at it in no time."

"That's the plan." I threw my arms out. "And this is the designated workshop space." I slid the barnwood panel behind us to reveal a back room. "This is going to be an office. I'll move the table and desk in here when I'm finished with the wiring." There was an architectural drawing of the building stabbed to the wall by two metal blades. "This is my plan."

Her fingers traced the outline of my building. "You're an architect too?"

"Nah, I just got photocopies of the original drawings and added my ideas."

Shay flicked the knives pinning the paper to the wall. "Nice thumbtacks." She wandered around the small office.

"They're a work in progress. You'll find that everything around here serves more than one purpose."

Her eyebrow quirked with curiosity. "Everything?"

"Yep, well just about." I walked toward the staircase leading to the second floor. I was out of my mind, thrilled to share my life. "Follow me." I ran, taking two steps at a time. I was eager to show off my ideas just as much as I was excited to have Shay right behind me. I kept pinching myself to prove it was real. "This is where I'm going to live."

"I guess you're safe now that the window's fixed?"

I turned around and gave her my most intense glare. "Really? You had to remind me."

"I am who I am, Wil."

"Ooh, good one." I pushed the garbage can out of our path. "We knocked out this half wall and opened up the floor space. The kitchen and living areas are here." We moved through the open room. "I've got an amazing claw-foot tub I found at a scrapyard. I'm almost done with the bathroom here, and the bedrooms are over there."

"This is a lot of work for one person."

"Not for me. I've got skills, Shay. I also have a few friends, and I called in some favors to make it habitable." I winked, and the smile I received in return fueled me through the rest of the tour.

"This is the coolest part." I pulled back one more sliding door to reveal the glass-covered frame.

"I saw your greenhouse during the search. I admit I'm a little jealous." She walked inside and dragged a hand across the chipping, painted framework.

"Don't be. My fingers work magic." I wiggled them in the air. "But my thumbs will never be green."

She picked up the bucket filled with potting soil, scooping the dirt with the tiny gardening trowel. "That's too bad. Maybe I can teach you how to use those thumbs?"

"If you remember, you're not the first one to try."

"No, I'm not." She snickered at the shared memory. "How could I ever forget?" She twirled another container on the table. "Your greenhouse reminded me of Mama Pierce right away."

"That's what I thought when I walked through here the first time." I took a deep breath. "Maybe, you could help me green up this little house, if you wanted?"

Her fingertip made a tiny heart in the glass. "I'd like that."

We stood in silence for a long moment. I wondered if Shay was remembering the same experience with the woman we called Mama. She walked to the edge of the greenhouse frame before breaking the silence. "I missed you, Wil." She drew a small *x* in the dirt on the glass. "I didn't know how much until I saw you this morning." She turned around. "I feel like that fifteen-year-old girl all over again."

"Standing in here with you, I'm feeling the same." I was nervous, shoving my hands in my pockets to hide the trembling. "A lot of things have changed. You got a little bit about me; I think it's your turn to catch me up on you." I held a hand to her and guided us back into the apartment.

We walked down to the first floor. The furniture was sparse, so I tipped over a couple of five-gallon plastic buckets. I slapped the top for hers to sit. A well-worn steel cooler separated us, and I reached inside. "Thirsty? I've got water, a couple of sodas, and a few beers."

She sighed, putting her hand out. "Beer me, please."

I tried not to stare at the palm of her hand. "Still my kinda girl." It was out of my mouth before I could stop myself.

Shay was casual in her response. "I guess, maybe. A lot has changed since we lived together . . ."

I came home from a counseling session to find my room empty. Shay was already gone, and it felt like I was being punished. The most painful part was that we didn't get to say goodbye. The look in Mama Pierce's eyes said everything.

"Wildwood, my dear, there's been a change in my status as a foster parent." That was the only explanation as her arms came around to hug me.

"Mama, I don't want to go." I could see a black plastic garbage bag in the hallway, and I knew everything I had was inside. I turned and ran out the back door and into the field behind the house. I threw myself to the ground and scrawled long lines in the dirt with my fingers, claiming the last memory of what felt like a home.

The social worker found me there. "Wildwood, it's time to go."

I wiped my hands on my pants before drawing my sleeve across my face to erase the tears that wouldn't stop. "I don't want to leave."

"There's nothing I can do to change it. We need to get on the road. It's a long drive to your new foster home."

That was the end of the discussion, and I had no power to change it. The strong arms of Mama Pierce wrapped around me in a loose hug. "Remember, you are who you are. Never apologize for it."

Shay's voice broke me from the memory. "That day, when they moved me, I didn't know what to do. I begged them to take me back, but they wouldn't. Before I knew it, I was in a home that didn't make sense and that I knew would last for less than a few months."

I regretted the direction of the conversation. "No one would tell me where you were," I said.

"I know. I tried to find you too, but we didn't have any power, did we?"

"I guess not." I popped the caps from the bottles of beer. "How exactly is it that you're a cop?"

"It was accidental."

I shook my head, not buying the casual attitude. "What, you tripped over a log and fell into that uniform?" I handed the drink to her and kicked my feet out, leaning against the wall behind me.

"Hardly." She took a long sip. "I turned seventeen, and I had nothing. I know you get that. I didn't know what to do or where to go, so I thought about the army. I went to a recruiting office, and the guy there was such a dick. I graduated high school six months later, which made Mama proud when I sent her the card." She took another sip of her drink. The sleeve of her shirt fell away from her wrist, revealing a scar on her arm.

I noticed, and before I could stop myself, I reached to touch the jagged skin. Shay pulled back, a conditioned response, which I could tell she regretted. I didn't turn away, wanting her to trust me with the memory.

"It's not what you think." Shay put down the beer and pulled back the cuff of both sleeves.

There was no way to prevent the gasp that escaped my mouth.

"Before I aged out . . . " Shay paused. "My last home was pretty rough."

I reached again but hesitated until she held her hands to me. My fingers trailed across the scars. "Hell, Shay. What happened?"

"It was a group home. I hated it before I even got out of the car." She rotated her shoulders, giving me the full view. "My roommate had night terrors and kept a knife under her pillow. No one knew about it until it was too late. She stabbed me fourteen times." Shay held her forearms up. "These are the scars that changed everything for me." I could tell that recalling the memory was painful. "Remember the thing we did in the field? That deep breathing and the energy work?"

I looked down at my own cherished scar, fearing I would burst into tears, and unable to find the correct words to say, my response was a silent nod.

"The doctor told me that the breathing exercise saved my life. In the middle of everything, I thought of you. I felt the blood running warm against my skin, and I thought I was back in the field with you. My heart rate slowed, and I closed my eyes." She let the memory come. "They thought I was dead, but I was in some kind of self-made coma."

Tears streamed down my cheeks. She survived because of one innocent moment. "I should have been there." I felt helpless. Nothing I could say or do would ever change the marks on her skin, but the damage to her trust was what scared me the most.

"No one knew." She rubbed the scars on her left arm. "We had no idea that Andi was so dangerous. The morning before she stabbed me, we'd joked about sneaking into the movies, eating popcorn and candy."

I wiped my face on the back of my arm. "And you became a cop because you got stabbed?"

She pulled her sleeves to cover the scars. "I became a cop because I survived being stabbed."

I was feeling a thousand different emotions, but her answer confused me. "Explain, please?"

Shay picked up the bottle and took a very long sip of her beer. "When I woke up a few days later—"

"A few days?" I interrupted.

"Breathe, Wildwood." We both took a long, calming inhale and exhale. "I slept for a few days. It was mostly because of the blood loss, but when I woke up, there was a detective there. She was kind in a way that made me suspicious, but after a few visits, I trusted her. I don't know why, but I did."

"So, instead of an army recruiter, you had a cop shop recruiter?"

"Not quite." She took the last sip of her drink. Her fidgeting reminded me of a caged animal. "Can we take a walk?"

My beer was almost full. "Sure." I left it on the table and followed her out the door, locking the shop behind us. "Lead the way."

Shay shoved her hands in her pockets and started to walk. I followed without concern about where we were going. I just wanted to know the rest of the story.

"Detective Reynold came every day until I was released, and she helped me get a room at a shelter. I told her about going into the military, but she said a fighter like me belonged on the streets of America." She led us to the city park. As the new kid in town, I trusted Shay to be my guide. "After, I applied for the academy. The great part was I had a place to live, and it turns out I'm good at being a cop."

"You were only eighteen?"

"Yep. I've been a cop for almost nine years now, and I wouldn't give it up for anything." She bumped my shoulder. "Tell me, where have you been staying?"

"Until recently I've been living in my car. I didn't want to get tied up while I was waiting for the carriage house."

"You can't live in your car." I could feel the intensity of her concern by the way she reacted.

I dangled my keys in front of Shay. "I don't have to anymore. I have a big beautiful building."

She snatched them out of my hand. The woman was quick. "With barely running water, and a half-functioning bathroom and sort of kitchen. You're keeping drinks in a cooler, for heaven's sake." She held out the keys in her palm. I reached for them, and she pulled away. She was toying with me, and I liked it.

"That's one hundred percent accurate, but it's temporary." She finally let me grab them.

"You hungry?" She leaned against the park bench. "I haven't eaten since this morning," she confessed.

I was watching the ducks in the river. "I could force down some food. Care to take me to your favorite restaurant? I'm kinda new around here."

Shay laughed at my silliness. "I know just the place. You still a ferocious carnivore?"

"A lot of things have changed, but that never will." I held out my hand to her. "Lead the way, boss."

Bannock was a small town, and we could walk most of the streets in a few hours. Shay pointed out her favorite pizza place and suggested I stay away from the restaurant claiming "authentic" American cuisine. I enjoyed the tour, but her company was the real treat. We stopped in front of an old building with cobblestone sidewalks. I looked up at the sign just before she stopped walking. "Slammed?"

"It's perfect. A total dive, but the food will knock you out." She opened the door for me.

The bar was one of the darkest pubs I'd ever been in, but it was rich with small-town history. The swooped-back chairs reminiscent of the Wild West surrounded the tiny round tables. A giant police badge fitted in the center of the wall, surrounded by mirrored bottles of alcohol. I stayed close to Shay until we reached a table. "Do you come here a lot?"

She was about to answer when arms closed around her neck. "You better be trained in hand-to-hand," Shay said as she winked at me, letting me know there was no real threat.

"I'd never beat you face to face." The woman planted a wet kiss on Shay's cheek, released the hold, and stepped into view. "What are you up to, kiddo?"

"Five eight the last time I checked."

The woman smiled, patting Shay's shoulder. "Hungry?"

"Starving." Shay held the hand for a few moments before making the introductions. "Regina Benton, this is a very old friend, Wildwood. Wil, this is Benton."

"The blacksmith?" I answered her question with a nod. "Call me Reggie or Benton. Regina sounds so old." She put out her hand.

"Field Training Officer Benton?" I reached to shake her hand, noticing a tiny tremor before she grabbed my own. "Nice to meet you."

Shay was impressed. "You always were a great listener."

"Nice to meet you. Very old friend? I think I've got boots older than the two of you combined." We laughed at the joke even though it wasn't amusing. "You need menus?"

Shay nodded. "Let's give her the full experience."

I didn't miss the wink and watched the old cop walk away. "Parkinson's?"

Shay looked over her shoulder, watching Reggie walk back to the bar. "Something like that, early stages maybe. She doesn't talk about it. She retired about two years ago. I miss her out there."

"This is her place?"

"The family owned it, and after she retired she took it over. She comes and goes a lot, leaving full-time staff here to run it."

I wasn't wholly comfortable with law enforcement. It wasn't that I was a criminal or had criminal inclinations but cops always came when things were terrible. "I'm guessing from the artwork behind the counter that this is a cop bar?"

"It's a bar, with cops, yes."

"I'm not sure I'll be comfortable here."

"Did you forget that I'm a cop?"

"Forget? That's impossible, but you're Shay. I'll always feel safe when I'm with you."

"Just like that?"

I shrugged. "I guess so."

I watched Benton approach the table, carrying a menu and two glasses of beer. "I figured this might hit the spot while you memorize our extensive dining options."

Shay laughed as I flipped the menu. "It's a burger joint," she explained.

"I see that." I turned the laminated cardstock over. "That serves a lot of beer."

Shay leaned in, resting her arms on the table. "Hence the name *Slammed*."

"It's all coming together now." I took a long sip of beer and reached to run my fingers through my hair. "Oh shit. I wasn't even thinking. Damn, I must look like a mess." I took off the hat, and a tangle of jet-black hair fell around my face.

"Actually, you look pretty wonderful."

I pointed a finger toward the entrance and the exit. "Bathroom is where?"

"Right over my shoulder. "

Dark hair flowing with every step, I pushed open the single-stall bathroom door. I saw my reflection in the mirror and laughed. "You look a fright, Blackstone." I stuffed the hat in my back pocket and turned on the water to wash my face. I finger-combed through the wild tangles that had been trapped under the work-stained cap. When I was satisfied I was presentable, I returned to the table. "Sorry about that."

"Not much has changed about you. You always got lost in what you were doing."

"You're right, not much has changed. Did you order some burgers?"

"Medium rare with fries."

We sat together, sharing stories. Shay offered more details about her position in the police department, and I expressed my excitement over the opportunity to restore the historic carriage house.

I wiped my lips on the napkin. "That was the best burger I've ever had."

I was adjusting to the way her smile traveled all the way to her eyes. "It's ridiculous, I know. I had to limit myself to once a week, or I'd have to add more time to my workout."

"I could fix that, you know."

"Could you, now?" Shay blushed for the first time, and it only made her more adorable.

I tried to erase the innuendo. "That's not what I meant."

Her elbows met the top of the table. "Please explain," she said, lacing her fingers together.

"I never work out. I don't have time, but I work hard. If you're looking for a real calorie burn, come over to the shop and help me finish building the upstairs apartment." I drank the last sip of my beer, satisfied that the challenge would create more time for the two of us to be together.

She shook her head. "That's pretty slick."

"What is?"

"The way that you just recruited me to work for nothing."

"Not nothing. For fitness."

Shay shook her head again. "I don't even know when I would fit hammering and sawing into my schedule."

Maybe it was the drink or just the personal memories we'd shared, but I was feeling bold. "You could start by drinking my beer instead of Benton's." I was beginning to believe that the universe loved me. What were the chances that the two of us would end up in the same small town?

She nodded in agreement. "How are you still single?"

I ran my fingers through my hair. "Why do you assume that I am?" I wiggled my eyebrows at her.

"Oh gosh, please don't do that." Shay laughed, reaching across the table to cover my forehead with her hands. "It's just not right."

I leaned back against the chair, crossing my feet at the ankles. "I am, by the way." I laced my fingers behind my head, waiting for her to respond.

"What?"

"Single."

I saw it in her eyes. She was too.

CHAPTER III

Welcome to Bannock

It was hard to believe, but there were still untamed mountains in this country. After a few weeks in this little city, I finally opened that packet I received when I got the keys to the carriage house. According to the documents, the tiny town of Bannock was a pioneer village abandoned after the rush for gold. In an attempt to attract tourism from the ghost-hunting community, the county planned to revive the old buildings, which led to their generous offer to me. If being in the right place at the right time was lucky, I found myself in the middle of absolute good fortune.

Shortly after the contract was offered, I rolled into the small town, and my application must have made it to the top of the pile. I understood how lucky I was, and I wasn't going to waste the opportunity. The old carriage house brought me to the rugged countryside, and back to the world I always believed I belonged. The most important part was that it brought me back to Shay—formerly Cortland—Pierce.

I was grateful I'd spent those long days with my friends, getting the building into livable condition. After they'd gone, I connected running water for my rustic bathroom and kitchen. It was a continuous work in progress, but that was temporary.

On an emergency call for repairs, I met Andrew, who ran a recycling company about thirty miles from Bannock. The place looked more like a junkyard, but he knew how to find just about anything on his property. His specialty: repurposed building materials, which was perfect for finding the fixtures I needed for the upper apartment.

In the morning, I earned my living repairing equipment for local businesses, and in the afternoon, I finished framing the space that was now my first home, but I was eager to be back at the forge.

The tiny town came with a reputation that I didn't research until the day Shay showed up to investigate my mysterious visitor. Strange things continued after our evening together. They were minor events at first: tools out of place, missing parts for the kitchen plumbing. Most I could explain away. When the energies of the workshop shifted beyond my ability to balance them, I called for help.

The reappearance of Shay in my life had been a perfect surprise. As per my suggestion, she showed up to drink my beer and help me work on the building. She paid attention, learning fast, which was helpful as we transformed the open space into a cozy apartment. I was comfortable inside the creaky old carriage house, but when I felt the creepiness of the old building, I called Shay.

She reminded me of the strong women who had helped raise us. I realized that I'd let my energy work fall to the side. I planned to reclaim that part of myself.

I was raking and grading the gravel floor in the corner of the workshop. The ground was unfinished, rough from centuries of keeping horses and animals in a building built on the edge of the industrial revolution. It was clear that my car was the only one ever parked inside. I groomed the dirt so I could lay forms for a concrete floor. It was a mix of gravel, sand, and shiny rocks that I thought might be pica.

I scooped up a pile of the mixture and threw it into my wheelbarrow. The icy change in the air was instant. The earth's energy shifted, throwing me off balance, and what I felt in this room was beyond anything I knew. I chanted, "Be of the light. Only light be near." I repeated it over and over as I pulled my phone from my pocket.

"Hello?"

"Shay?" I asked.

"What's up, Wil?"

I turned around in the space, trying to determine what I was feeling. "Some weird shit."

"What do you mean by 'weird shit'?"

I could hear the background noise of her police radio. "When you've got a minute, come by my shop, would you?"

"Give me a few."

"Is that minutes or hours?"

"That's funny. I guess it depends on if it's weird shit or really weird shit."

I could picture the smile on her face even though Shay wasn't beside me. "It's really weird. You should get here as quick as you can, please."

As it happened, Shay was patrolling the area a few blocks from the carriage house and arrived before I had time to unlock the entrance. She was beating her fist against the peeling paint, knocking white flakes to the ground.

I opened the door, and we were face to face. "That was quick."

"You said 'really weird' shit, so I'm here. What's going on?"

I was breathless as I led her to the spot where I'd been working. "I know that this is not police procedure, but you need to trust me and close your eyes, Shay."

"Am I going to regret this?" The room felt cold, and she stepped closer to me.

"Close your eyes, woman. You need to feel, not see." In the few weeks since reconnecting, we'd spent hours talking about our year together, finding our way through the uncertain times to understand the women we'd grown to be. Shay hadn't forgotten the peace that came from her life with Mama Pierce and with me. Knowing that she felt the same about all of those stolen moments made me want to be with her even more. For the first time, my future was abundant with possibilities, and I thought I understood what it was to find and make a stable life.

On an 80-degree day, the room shouldn't have felt like ice. "Is it good or evil?" she asked.

"So you feel it?" I lit a match and touched it to the taper candle.

"I'm not sure what I feel." She held her hands out as if reading the room with her palms.

I rotated a bundle of sage in the flame, paying close attention to the rise of smoke. The thin line drifted toward the west end of the building as I followed the edge of the rock floor. "Definitely not good." My movement was slow, purposeful, allowing the thin ribbon to collect and break the heavy energy in the room. "I'm beginning to think that my visitor might be from an alternate place."

Shay stood in the center of the room, watching me fan the sage. "Have you seen anything since we were here on that first day?"

I shook my head as the smoke transformed from a thin ribbon into a billowing cloud. "Seen? No. It's always just a feeling, like someone is beside me, but there's never anyone there. It's smoking out. Whatever is here, I think I need to do some research. Have you ever heard anyone talk about ghosts in here?"

Shay broke the tension in the room with a burst of laughter. "This whole town is literally a ghost town. I have to believe that the building that was the central location for most of the business might have had some negative happenings."

"Negative happenings? So that's a yes and the understatement of the year." The thin ripples coming from the burning bundle began to spread. The transformation meant that the energies of the room had shifted. "It feels like this is working. Come here, please."

In her uniform, Shay was a presence. The bulletproof vest under her shirt hid the feminine curves of her body, but I still knew they were there. She adjusted the radio on her hip and responded to the call that broke the silence. "This is Pierce. I'm ten twenty-three. Will update by phone."

I handed the smoking bundle to her. "Keep walking around the outside edge. When the smoke starts to collect, move forward."

"I know how to smudge, Wil." She grabbed the smoldering herbs and followed the path around the room. "Are you that freaked out?"

My hair fell around my face as I lit the second bundle of sage. "I'm not." The candle flame flashed high and turned blue just before an unexpected shift of air forced us into darkness. The embers crackled, reflecting light in my eyes and hers.

Shay caught a glimpse of surprise on my face as the room went still. She turned on her flashlight, casting the beam in my direction.

"Don't move." I was reaching for the flint striker as my hand spun the valve on the gas line to the forge. The propane made a sucking sound as flames burst out the open ends of the huge fireproof box. With the insulated door open, the gas burned bright enough to fill the room.

The shadows lingered in the corner as Shay shined her light to fill them. "You see that, Wil?"

It was moving at us with little time to react. Shay drew her baton and extended it with a flick of her wrist. The first strike hit hard and knocked the creature on the side of its head. I picked up the shovel and struck at full force before it could recover. "What the hell is it?"

Its eyes flared with a golden reflection of the forge's light. My second strike of the shovel forced the creature back, slamming its head into the flaming box. The scent of burning monster hit us as the sound of the screeching creature filled the room. "This can't be real."

"Sorry, Wil. Welcome to Bannock." Shay dropped her baton and drew the taser from her duty belt. "Take that, you son of a bitch." The flash grazed the creature. Letting out a sound I'd never heard before, it scurried up the wall, across the ceiling, and out the open door.

I struggled to catch my breath. The forge flashed a bright white flame that burst from its open ends, forcing both of us off our feet and to the ground. The gas hissed without a flame, and I shuffled across the floor to shut the valve. I watched Shay stand and clap the dirt from her uniform. "Tell me what the hell just happened," I yelled.

Shay was on her radio, calling dispatch. "Pierce to base. Class-two encounter at my location. I'll be ten seven, code five. I'll call in with an update." She felt my hand on her shoulder and turned to look at me.

"Tell me what the hell just happened, Shay!"

She was deep in cop mode, directing the beam of her flashlight around the room. She lingered over the reflection in the freshly grated dirt. "Shit!" She flicked her wrist, strobing the flashing beam, making the ground shimmer.

What and who was the person in front of me? I was confused by more than just the creature attack. The woman I thought I knew suddenly morphed into a hunter of what could only be . . . monsters. "What do you mean 'shit'?"

Shay bent down and sifted her fingers through the gravel, sorting out the shimmering pieces. She scooped up a handful and plucked out the pebble-sized sparkly bits. "Shit."

"Will you stop saying that?" I grabbed the flashlight from her hand so I could find the circuit box on the wall. It was old, and as I surveyed the fuses, I made a mental note to get the service updated. I twisted the tube and replaced it with a new one. The lights turned on, and I watched as Shay dropped her handful of pebbles into a plastic vial. "Will you please tell me what's going on?"

The sample reacted with the solution at the bottom of the tiny container. "Salt."

"Salt in the dirt?" I grabbed her shoulder. "What does that have to do with the damn thing that just attacked us?"

She shoved the glass vial in her pocket before standing. "I think you better sit down, Wil. What I'm about to tell you might be a lot to take in."

Thoughts were bouncing around in my mind, and I turned to walk away. It was clear that Shay understood more than me and that this wasn't the first time she'd fought a thing I couldn't even define. I grabbed the railing of the staircase and dragged myself up to the second-floor apartment. It was still a work in progress, but the thrift store table and chairs were better than the upturned buckets from our first day together in Bannock. I grabbed a beer from the cooler, popped the top, and fell into the chair. "I'm sitting down. Why don't you tell me what the hell just happened?"

She took a deep breath. "You aren't here by accident, Wil." Shay turned off the police radio on her hip. She unclipped the lapel mic and pulled on the buckle of her duty belt, oblivious to how I might feel watching her strip out of her uniform or the effects of this new reality.

"What do you mean?"

"First, please let me say that this isn't how I planned to tell you and that I hope you'll still feel the same about me after you understand what's been going on."

"Just . . ." I looked in her eyes. "Tell me."

"That." She pointed to the workshop below us. "You just had your first encounter with a class-two demon." She waited for me to hear and process her words. I didn't know how to react as she continued. "This sample from the corner downstairs has salt in it." She held up the tiny vial. "I'm pretty sure that the floor that you've been grading was the location of a containment circle, and you destroyed it when you shoveled out the dirt."

"You're telling me this like it's nothing, like you've done this before." She peeled away everything that identified her as a cop. She ripped at the velcro from the front of her vest and dropped it next to her duty belt. She stood in front of me, wearing khaki pants and a dark short-sleeved V-neck undershirt. It was the first time I could see all of the scars on her arms.

"That's because I have."

I finished my beer and reached for another. "So a class-two demon"—I pointed at Shay for confirmation of the proper name — "who was stuck in a circle of salt just attacked us. I fried half of its head in the forge, and it still ran away?"

She was rubbing her arms. I could tell by her discomfort that she rarely let anyone see them. "That about sums it up, but I've got a confession to make."

"Another one?" I was having a difficult time with the words coming out of her mouth, struggling to keep my composure. "Let me guess. You're not a regular beat cop?" I took a savoring sip of my fresh beer and swished it around my tongue before swallowing.

Shay nodded. "I'm a regular cop who happens to fight demons too. That's why I'm in Bannock. It's mostly because of meeting you."

I pinched my arm, making sure that the last few minutes weren't part of a terrible nightmare. Demons weren't real. How were any of the words coming out of Shay real? I was skeptical about everything I'd just experienced, wanting to shut out this new reality. I kicked off my shoes and pulled my feet up to my chest. "I think you should rewind and start from the beginning."

Shay draped her uniform over the chair. I could see the dark scars peppering her forearms. "Are you sure you should take your vest off?"

"It's only good for human weapons." She raised a curious pointed finger. "You aren't going to pull one on me?"

If the events of the evening hadn't happened, I might have found her joke funny, but it was too soon. "I guess it depends on what comes out of your mouth in the next couple of minutes."

Shay untucked her undershirt and reached toward the cooler. "You mind if I have one?"

"I guess you're off duty since your superhero costume is all over my kitchen."

"Super, I am not." The shift of power was noticeable as she stripped out of her uniform. I glimpsed the girl I thought I knew. She was vulnerable, and the first signs of fear were clear. She rolled the ice-covered can across her forehead. "Do you remember when we were kids, and you taught me about the earth and energy work?" Shay's voice broke as she asked the question. I assumed that she felt the same as I did, but in this moment, everything that I knew was skewed.

I rubbed the scar on the palm of my hand. "Is that a real question? Because I could never forget that . . . or us."

"It changed me, Wil. The more you shared, the more I wanted to know. So I studied. After the social worker moved me from you and Mama, I thought I wanted to give up. It almost killed me to be away from you." The sweat on her forehead was masked by the water droplets left behind as she swiped the beer can across her brow. "But we promised." She avoided making eye contact with me. "My heart ached for you in a way that I didn't understand. I know now that it was love. I get that I fell in love with you, but that wasn't the only part. The way we connected, it was spiritual, something not of this world, and I can feel it still, even after all of this time."

"What does that have to do with the thing that attacked us downstairs?"

"When I moved into the home—" She paused to rub the scars on her forearm. "Right before this happened." She held up the wounds as if I wasn't already looking at them. "I started to read everything I could about what we did together. I studied pagan rituals and the religion of Wicca until I could recreate what happened to me in that field. I wanted it all back. If I couldn't have you, I was going to keep the one thing that connected us."

I released the breath I didn't know I was holding. My beer was empty, and before opening another, I needed complete clarity when I asked my next question. "Did you bring me here to Bannock?" Shay nodded. "Because you needed me or because you needed my help?"

"Yes, and yes," she replied.

Frustrated and hurt, I dragged my fingers through my hair. I felt the dirt that collected on my scalp from the weird encounter in my shop. "You know, if you'd told me you loved me before all of this happened, I might be kissing you right this very second."

"But?"

I let out a defeated sigh. "But I feel slightly betrayed and used."

For the first time in all of our moments together, I saw fear in her eyes. "Wil, that's not at all what I intended." She dropped down in the chair beside me, looking as exhausted as I felt.

"Enlighten me, Shay." I was rubbing the scar on my palm.

"I guess it can't get worse." She finished her beer and crushed the can. She wiggled the tab back and forth until it broke away. "Eight months ago, when the city council was going through the applications for the carriage house, I was at the meeting." She shot the can across the room and into the recycle bin. It was a momentary distraction until she turned to look at me. "We'd just finished a hearing about getting a K-9 unit, so I stuck around to see what was going to happen with the award. They discussed the final three applicants, and when I heard your name, I interrupted to add what I could about you. I know I'm young, but my experience and my opinion hold weight in this town. I explained how we knew each other, how we shared a foster home. The council vote was almost unanimous. So I guess if it wasn't for me, you might never have ended up in this haunted, demon-filled ghost town."

I felt a chill in the air and reached around to cover my arms. "It's impossible to think otherwise. You know what?" I didn't give her time to answer. "I was excited about the carriage house. I thought . . ." I pulled my hair into a bunch and fiddled with the ends before releasing it around my face. "I thought I'd finally proven that I was enough."

Shay shook her head, reaching to take my hand. "You are enough. You're everything."

I looked down at our fingers tangled together, and it was impossible to forget where we'd been. "So you're a demon hunter." I squeezed her hand. "What happens now?

"I'll make a few phone calls and talk to Bent and the chief. They have more experience with the ethereal world than I do."

"Not with the demons. I'm not even close to believing what happened tonight. I meant what happens with us?"

I felt her body tense as her grip on my hand released. "I guess that depends on you."

I wasn't a quitter, but the person sitting beside me had shattered my world to pieces. "You scare the hell out of me, Shay."

"I don't mean to," she whispered.

"I can see that."

Anyone in their right mind would run from the carriage house, from Bannock, and maybe even from Shay. I wanted to load up my life and go, but this was the dream. If I knew one thing about dreams, it was that they never came easy. "So the sample from my floor, what does that mean for my carriage house?"

She rubbed the scars on her forearm. "I guess it means that you've got some demon activity at the very least."

"And at the very most?"

"The carriage house is a portal to hell?"

My eyes went wide as I covered my mouth to stifle the curse words forming. "Portal to hell? are you serious?" It was the worst timed joke in the history of joke telling, and I wanted to punch her in the face. But she wasn't joking.

"That's the worst-case scenario." She shook the vial in front of her. "I'll take this back to the station. They'll analyze the remnants, and I'll do some research based on what they find."

"So, you are a superhero?"

"You need to stop with that. I'm just a cop doing my job."

Everything I thought I knew about Shay was turned around. She wasn't frail or fragile. She'd turned the violation of her body into an opportunity to become stronger. The student had become my teacher, and as much as I wanted to be angry, I was also impressed. "I don't believe it's that simple, not for a single minute, hero."

"You have to stop. I'm no kind of hero."

"I guess time will tell." I threw my crushed can in the recycle bin. "What kind of research do you do?"

Shay picked up her shirt and vest and slid her belt over her shoulder. "I can show you if you're interested."

"I've never wanted to know anything as much as I want to know what you've been up to for the last ten years." I led her down the stairs and followed her to the squad car. The trunk popped open by remote, and I stopped. "Your squad car is possessed too?"

"You're kidding, right?"

"I am. I just thought it was funny that you'd open the trunk before we were out the door. Don't you have equipment back there?"

"I do, but it's safe."

"Care to explain?"

"I guess that leads me back to our conversation upstairs. I felt the power between us when we were girls. I've learned how to be in that power, but I've also learned quite a bit more." Shay dropped her gear in the back of the car and opened a case that was in the trunk. She pulled out a pile of books and a thick leather-bound tome. "This is what I've been doing. This is me, I guess."

I took the stack from her arms before she closed the trunk of her car. I carried everything back into the building, watching the dark corners more than I ever had before.

She was standing at the door. "You don't have to be paranoid when we're together. I'll know if something shows up again."

I set the stack of papers and her tome on my worktable, and I moved to watch her go. "How will you know?"

She stopped and turned to look at me. "I think that's a story for another night." She winked at me. "Read the books." And then she was gone.

CHAPTER IV

Partners

It had been less than twenty-four hours since the demon encounter and a few short weeks since Shay had returned to my life. I had mixed feelings about my new reality. I fought to separate fact from fiction, and the giant demon tome on my makeshift table brought more confusion than answers. The book was divided into four sections, each explaining the classes of creatures and how to deal with them.

"Demons?" It didn't seem possible, and I thought that reading it out loud would make it real. "Class-one demons have a killing poison, venom, or biologically attached weapon. They kill or harm for no reason." I turned the page to see sketches of indescribable beings, diagrams of their connected weapons, and killing strength. "This reads like a damn gaming manual. How is this even real?" I closed the book, deciding that getting messy in the forge would be the perfect distraction.

After the ethereal invasion, the energy in my workshop had shifted. The space didn't feel like my own. I hoped that a few hours of sweat-filled fun would change it. I put on my gloves. I always wore them when I worked. Hot or cold, the space was dangerous, and my hands made everything happen. I grabbed the broom from the corner and swept the mess that our short encounter created. I wasn't thinking about what I would make. I was just hoping to get lost in the rhythm of blacksmithing. I vacuumed the base of the forge and double-checked the short propane tank beside it. I made a plan to install a permanent setup, with a monthly delivery of gas. I couldn't do that until the contractors poured cement for the floor. I glanced over at the graded patch of rock. *This can't be my reality*, I thought to myself.

I checked the gas line connected to the top of the forge and noticed the strange distortion in the blackened fireproof box. "What the hell?" I touched the melted glob that was hanging halfway out. It felt solid, but not like any material I'd worked with in the past. It didn't make sense for it to be there after our epic demon battle. I laughed as I grabbed a set of tongs to tap on the mystery metal. It popped from the edge, and I picked it up. It was more substantial than it looked, and I wondered if it was a demon leftover.

I took off my gloves, hoping to feel the energy inside this demon remnant. Repurposing material wasn't uncommon in the world of blacksmithing. Finding odd bits of scrap and making them into something new was part of the excitement. "I wonder if class-two demons turn to metal when you heat them to two thousand degrees?" The words came out of my mouth as I closed my eyes. It was cold in my hands and most like the feeling of desolation that I'd ever touched. I wasn't sure that energy work on a burnt demon was a good decision. I put my gloves back on, deciding that handling demons with my bare hands should be limited.

I laughed, deciding to experiment with this new find. I opened the propane valve and squeezed the igniter. The sparks hit the gas, and the sound of the sucking flame filled the quiet space. Even though the fire was instant, it would take a minute to get to temperatures that soften steel. I set the clump of metal against the belt of the grinder. I thought of Shay and our first encounter in this ghost-and-demon-filled town. *Mysterious visitor turned ghost turned demon. No one would ever believe it.*

It was common practice, when repurposing metal, to check the hardness by grinding the edge against a belt sander. This particular piece made sparks that lit the ground, and my leather apron, on fire. I had no idea why it went from spark to flame, but if I could forge an edge to this material, it would be the fiercest weapon for anyone to wield.

"You feeling lucky?" I spoke to no one in particular as I used tongs to place the blob into the fiery box. I put on my safety glasses and watched as it changed from cold gray to blazing orange and then to the hot white of welding temperature. I pulled it from the flames and placed it against the anvil. My first strike came with a measure of hesitation, but when my hammer met the demon remnants, the sound was like the echo of death. I'd never heard anything like it. "What the hell?"

High-carbon steel sounded like a chain rattling against itself. I've heard it for years, and for me, it's a bit like music. Demon steel was very different. I hammered the material until the shape was close to a standard billet, something comparable to the handle of a broom. The more I hit it, the less it howled. It fit well in my tongs as I placed it back into the fire. As a blacksmith, the force and angle of my hammer strike shaped the material and every impact on typical projects left behind tiny bits of impurity known as scale. It was usual for a measured cup to collect on the floor under the anvil. I worked this billet for an hour. Nothing fell to the ground. I realized I had a lot to learn about working demon steel.

While the piece was flaming hot, I chiseled off a three-inch chunk to keep for future testing. I continued to work for hours, hammering out two identical punch-style daggers. I didn't have an excellent selection of supplies for handles, so I settled on a few pieces of bone. It was durable, and if this blade was as hard as I thought it would be, it would need to feel tight in my grip. I shaped the handle to fit in my hand. I polished the blade, honing the edge until it was razor-sharp. Testing a finished creation was the reward for hard work. As much as I loved the creative part, testing it was just as fun. I pulled a piece of paper from my recycle bin and drew the blade against the edge. The page burst into flames as it sliced through. The knife was sharp, but it was also something else.

I was hesitant to talk to Shay about this experiment, but I was wise enough to know that I should. My blades had the potential to push dangerous to the extreme. I laid the matching daggers on the table before making the dreaded call.

"Hello?"

Her voice made me feel like a teenager. "Officer Pierce?"

"Wildwood?"

"Yes, it's me." I wasn't ready to let go of my feelings about her deception, and I didn't want to need her help. I was frustrated, but my choices were limited, and this time I'd have to concede. "I have something to show you. When you've got a minute, could you come by the shop?"

"I'm not on the clock today, so let me finish what I'm working on and I'll be over."

She had me thinking about a thousand different things she might be doing. I played guessing games in my head as I stitched together a simple belt-looped sheath for her knife. I knew her experience with blades and the injuries she carried would make her feel uneasy. I thought wrapping the edge would help.

As it turns out, I had plenty of time to finish covering both daggers. I was ambidextrous but I liked a knife in my left hand. I tucked mine on my hip. I was pulling it out to test the sheath when she knocked on the door. There she was, standing with one hand in her pocket and the other connected to a short tether with a beautiful German Shepard on the end. I still had the knife in my hand. The dog saw me as a threat and was barking, pulling the leash taught.

"Dexter, heel!" There was no missing the authority in Shay's command, and the dog's butt dropped to the ground. It was silent, but I wasn't about to make a move. "You might want to put down your knife," she said.

My movement was slow and deliberate as I tucked the blade back into the sheath. "Sorry, I was just checking the fit when you knocked. You caught me off guard."

"I seem to be making a habit of catching you off guard."

I opened the door for the two of them to enter, Dexter sticking close to her left side. She looked casual in a T-shirt and jeans. The sleeves on the flannel she wore were rolled, revealing the scars on her arms. I wanted to see them. I was curious for a thousand reasons, but most of all, I just wanted to know everything about her.

"Did you get the guard dog for me or because of me?" I didn't know why I asked such a stupid question. Maybe it was nerves or just breaking the very thick ice that had formed overnight.

She laughed. "Dex is my new partner."

"The K-9 unit, at the meeting, that was for you?"

"Yep. We've been training together for the last few months. Dexter passed his test, and now we are partners, one hundred percent official."

"That's cool. Does he get a uniform like yours?" I wasn't much of a dog lover. In fact, I didn't have much need for pets. They kept you anchored, and until moving to Bannock, I had no desire to stay in one place for very long. My first thought as I looked at this animal, was that he was big. His paws matched the size of my hands. His head came well past Shay's waist when he was sitting beside her. Our conversation was awkward, and I knew it. I didn't want to hold a grudge, but I felt the sting of betrayal. Shay led me to this town. She dragged me into a crazy demon-filled world, and I didn't understand any of it.

"I've been fundraising for the last few months to get him a vest." Her hand fluffed the long hair between his black-and-brown ears. He lifted his nose, guiding Shay's hand to pet his face. He seemed as attached to this woman as I was.

"Bulletproof and ready to bite?"

"Something like that."

"Doesn't the department supply your gear?" The who, what, and why of law enforcement was another language to me. I'd had limited exposure, but from my experience, cops showed up when a foster home was in chaos. If I wanted to spend any time with this pair, I'd have to learn to trust them beyond the veil of the uniform.

"You'd be surprised what they don't supply." Shay unclipped the leash and left her dog to wander in the shop. "So you called me, what's up."

"First, I want you to take a look at what I made today."

We stood side by side in front of my worktable. The punch dagger was sheathed, with only the grip exposed. The handle was vertical to the blade, looking like a large *T*. She didn't touch it. "You made a knife?"

"I made two, actually. One for me and one for you." I unfastened my belt, removing the weapon from my hip. I wasn't about to have a repeat of the ferocious barking from Dexter. I laid them side by side and, except for the coloring of the bone, they were a matched pair. I let her explore them and watched as she removed the guarding sheaths.

"These are beautiful." Her finger touched the mark I'd hammered into the blade. "This is your logo?"

"It's called a maker's mark. It's a way to identify me as the creator. It's a business card that won't get lost." Shay raised her left eyebrow with a questioning glare. I conceded. "Yes, it's also my logo."

"And it looks a bit like your wrist tattoo?" She pointed to my arm.

"Yep." My response was a little too enthusiastic.

"You called me over to look at knives?"

"I called you over to look at them, yes, but there's a story." I pulled out a new piece of paper from the recycle. "You might want to take a step back." She moved away and, a few seconds later, watched as I sliced the page, and it burst into flames.

"Is it flint? I don't understand."

I shook my head, my eyes wild with excitement. "It's demon."

She reached to grab her blade and held it in her hand. "What do you mean, 'it's demon'?"

I watched her sweep the dagger through the air. I could tell she liked how it felt in her hand. "Maybe you should sit down, and I think you should leave the knife on the table." I was nervous about explaining what I'd done with the demon metal. "I was reading your magick tome this morning."

"That's good. Were you trying to make a demon-killing weapon? What is this called, by the way?"

"It's a punch dagger. I've made quite a few. They're popular with my martial arts customers, and I can also modify them for hunters to use for skinning animals."

"I only use knives in my kitchen." Her eyes glanced down to her hands. "I'm sure you get why."

I was hesitant to admit my passion for bladesmithing. "It's how I've made a living for the last few years. I'd sell this pair for about six hundred dollars. That's with the sheathes."

"I had no idea."

I shrugged my shoulders. "Why would you?"

"Tell me, what did you learn from the tome?" She changed the subject. I was grateful.

"Wait here," I said. My movement was quick, and Dexter responded by running to Shay's side.

"Heel, Dex." The dog was obedient, and I made a mental note to use slower movements until we got to know each other better. It was hard enough to adjust to Shay, and now I had to learn to be around her dog. I walked to the table and grabbed the book. I opened it to the class-two section and laid it in front of us.

"When I said it was demon, I meant it was *actually* made from a demon. Last night, when we had that encounter, and the thing's head hit the forge, some kind of stuff was left behind."

"Stuff?" Her expression was not encouraging. In fact, it bordered on scolding.

I knew I was telling the story too slow, but I wasn't sure how to explain what I found and why I decided it was a good idea to forge these weapons. "The tome was overwhelming. When I get like that, I go to the forge to hammer it out. Today, when I was setting up to work, I found something dripping from it."

She interrupted me. "Dripping?"

"It's the best way to describe it. When I hit it with my tongs, it sounded and felt like metal."

"And you thought, 'I guess I'll make some knives'?"

I shrugged my shoulders. "Yeah, I kinda did."

She was shaking her head as I flipped the blade over on the table. "I tested it on the grinder, and when it sparked, the floor started on fire."

"So you thought it was a great idea to make knives?"

I smiled and let out a little laugh. "Lots of sparks means that the material is very hard. I figured, if it almost started concrete on fire, the blades would be unbreakable?"

Her brow furrowed with disapproval. "This might be the most reckless thing I've ever seen."

"Says the demon-hunting cop." I looked at her and her panting partner. "I'm about to pull a knife, and I don't want you to react, and I certainly don't want Dexter to rip my arm off. Could you hold on to him?"

"Dexter, here." She called the dog to her side. He walked over and put his head in her lap. She clipped the lead to his collar and held it tight.

"When I made this blade . . ." I pulled it from the sheath, and Dexter's ears stood up. "When I stuck it in the forge, it acted like steel. I let it get white-hot, and the first time I hit it with my hammer, it howled." I couldn't determine if Shay's expression was disapproval or disbelief. I continued. "Each time I struck it, the howling got quieter. The metal was silent once the blades were shaped." She was shaking her head as I spoke. "I struck my mark and attached the handle material. The entertaining part was removing the hammer marks and honing the edge." I held up my apron. "It's a good thing this is resistant to flame."

"Is it?" She ran a hand over the charred leather. "It looks like you fell in a campfire."

"At times, it felt like I did too." I grabbed a piece of leather left over from making the sheath. I pushed my blade through it, and the material flamed. "It doesn't matter what I cut or punch. It flames." I hit the steel drum behind me. When I withdrew it, the metal was smoking. I struck a concrete block. Once the fire was out, the slice left behind looked like a saw blade had cut right through. "It's impossible to break."

"I don't understand. I've never seen anything like this." Shay was holding her blade again. "Did you figure out what kind of demon it was?"

I shook my head at her. "Everything happened so fast. I'm not sure I remember anything about it."

Shay was already thumbing through her book. I attached my knife back on my belt, waiting for her to find some answers. "When you pushed the demon into the forge, what caught fire?"

"I'm pretty sure it was the head."

"When it came out, did it still have both horns?" She stopped on the page that looked like the monster from our waking nightmare. She held up the picture.

I nodded. "That's it."

"According to this, it's a gatekeeper. *Huic ostiarius* is a class-two demon." She skimmed over the text. "I don't see anything about liquifying into metal or howling guts."

I was distracted by the way the creature's name rolled off her tongue. "Latin?"

Her smile was adorable. "It comes with the job description."

"Demon-speak one oh one standard police academy training?"

"Something like that."

I picked up her knife by the blade. "Will you hold it in your hand?" I was trying to be sensitive to her history, but I wanted her to feel what I did when I used it. I held it to her. She hesitated before letting it rest in her palm. Her fingers curled around the bone of the handle. I looked at her hands, and I looked at mine. They weren't alike at all, but somehow the weapon fit.

"I thought it would be heavier." She stabbed the air in front of her and flexed her fingers to adjust the grip.

"It's nothing I've ever worked with, so I can't even explain it." I was pleased to see her connect with my creation. I'd made hundreds of blades, but never anything so unique. "But you like it?"

Shay walked toward the workshop; Dexter was at her side before she took a step. She picked a stone from the pile in the corner and pushed the blade deep. There was no hesitation as it penetrated, splitting the rock in half. "What's not to like?" The dog's ears perked as the flaming pieces flopped away.

"What do you think this means?" I had a thousand questions, and the woman in front of me wasn't answering any.

"I think this means that we need to have a conversation with Benton." Shay tucked the knife blade into its sheath and slid it in her back pocket before dialing the number on her cellphone. "Benton, it's Shay. We've got something we need to talk to you about. You around?" I could only hear Shay's side of the conversation, but it sounded like we were going for a walk. "Yep, we'll be there in a few." She ended the call. "Benton says, come now. It's not very busy at the bar."

"Let me lock up the shop, and we can walk over. I'm pretty sure I'll want a beer." I put my tools away. I was aware that her eyes followed me around the building. "I wouldn't be offended if you helped me." Shay was an intriguing enigma. She was confident, not arrogant, but guarded in a way that I didn't understand yet.

"I'd rather stand here and watch." She crossed her arms, leaning against the open door.

I pushed through the sleeves of my flannel shirt. "So watching is your thing."

"First and foremost, I'm trained to be an observer, but it's not always satisfying."

She made me laugh and smile and feel like I could forget the world. "Maybe we can discuss that later."

"Maybe we should." She was outside before I could respond, Dexter following close. I locked the door behind us, and we walked to the bar. The air was fresh as the sun was setting. Shay looped Dexter's leash around her wrist and pulled the knife from her pocket. "Have you cut any flesh with this?"

I huffed at the suggestion. "No. I'm pretty good at not bleeding when I work."

"That's not what I meant. I was just wondering if it cauterizes when it slices skin." She was flicking the edge of the blade, testing the sharpness against her thumb.

Her question was curious, one that I hadn't considered. "I'm not sure. Maybe we can try it out on a burger?"

"Maybe. I'll ask Benton if we can test it on something raw and already dead." She sheathed the knife just before we arrived. I'm sure she had her reasons, but she hid the blade in the long side pocket of her jeans. We stood in the arched foyer. Benton met us at the door, and I noticed the bar was a little crowded. She rubbed her hand on the top of Dexter's furry head, palming the dog a crunchy treat.

"If you keep that up, he's going to expect them every time we come in." Shay tightened her grip on the leash. We followed Benton to a quiet table in the back. It was evident by the way we moved through the crowd that they'd met to talk about demon adventures before. The dog was under the table as if he'd been in the pub his entire life.

"So what's the big news?" Benton rubbed her hands together like a kid at Christmas, eager to see the surprise. Shay laid her knife on the table. I took mine out of the sheath and handed it to the retired cop.

"Wildwood made this out of something we can't identify."

Benton fought to hide her tremors as she studied the dagger. "Why can't you identify it?"

"It might have been left behind after we tangled with a class two."

Benton set the blade on the table. "You tangled with a two, and something was left behind? Maybe you should rewind and start this story from the beginning."

Shay and I took turns detailing our encounter from the night before, although her side had more technical points and a lot of Latin. Benton didn't say a word. She just stood from the table and disappeared for what seemed like forever.

"Where'd she go?" I was concerned we were in trouble.

As if he could sense a change in the mood, Dexter put his head in Shay's lap. "I have no idea, but she gets like this sometimes. Like I said before, she's got a lot of experience chasing demons."

Benton returned to the table, carrying three beers in one hand and a raw piece of meat in the other. "Let's see what it does to that." I had to admit the test excited me, but I let Shay do the honors. She drew the blade across the thick steak. I expected to smell burning flesh, but instead, it produced a cleanly sliced piece of raw meat. "It's sharp at least."

"All of my knives are." I didn't know Benton well enough to understand that most of her thoughts came right out of her mouth.

"I wonder why it didn't burst into flames?"

After taking a long sip of her beer, Benton left the table again. Her unpredictable back and forth was unnerving, and I wished she would fill us in on what she was doing. She was gone long enough for us to finish our drinks and slice that meat into tiny bits. Shay fed a few to the dog under the table. Benton balanced the second round of drinks on top of a ragged binder and a stack of files. She cleared off our dishes and spread the papers across the tabletop. My shiny punch dagger lay in the middle.

"This was the flesh of a *Huic ostiarius*, a gatekeeper." There was no question in her tone.

Shay nodded and pointed to the pencil-sketched creature. "It happened so fast, but I came to the same conclusion."

She shuffled through the pages again. "They're class two all the way, but if you look through these notes, there's not one word about metal flesh that howls." Reggie slapped her hand on top of the notes. "Wildwood Blackstone, I want to shake your hand. You might have just changed the face of demon police work for Shay. I'm going to put a lot of emphasis on the 'might have' though."

"Benton, be serious. What are you talking about?"

"Shay, I've been doing this since I was your age, and believe me when I say this is special."

"So, I'm a demon blacksmith?"

Shay crossed her arms over her chest. "That's not a thing." She shook her head and glared at Benton. "Is it a thing?"

She chuckled at Shay's reaction. "Apparently, it is now, and your friend here is about to get the chance to prove her skills."

I had a lot of respect for Shay, and I trusted her relationship with this retired cop, but I wasn't sure I wanted anyone telling me how and when to work. "I'm a simple person, Benton. I don't need much. I keep my head down, and when it's time to be creative, I follow my own path. Honestly, I don't want to be your test dummy. I'm also not that excited to smelt demon into metal."

Shay leaned against the back of her chair. I could see her boots cross at the ankle under the table. Up until this moment, she hadn't acted this casual, and not this relaxed. She finished her second beer and put her hand on mine. "You won't have to do it alone."

I felt the squeeze, but she didn't release. Nothing I could remember ever felt as comfortable as her hand in mine. "I've been on my own for way too long. It's a hard habit to break."

Benton started piling the papers back into a folder. "I'm going to make a couple of phone calls and have a few things sent over to Shay's house."

"Things?" I didn't like the vague description.

She smiled at us, and the message in her expression said it all. "I may have a collection of demon bits. I want you to throw them in your forge, and tell me what you get."

"As exciting as it sounds, I'm not sure I want to do that."

Without warning, Shay dropped some cash on the table, hugged her friend, clipped Dexter to his leash, and held her hand to me. "Let's go for a walk, Wil."

She wasn't asking me, and I should have been offended by the command, but after all we'd been through, I still believed in her. Having faith in others didn't come easy, and that was as much a scar to my humanity as the wounds Shay carried on her arms. We stepped outside, and the sun had set. The moon was full, lighting the dark corners of the small town. I knew an intense conversation was coming, and I waited . . . for Shay.

Shay hooked her hands on her pockets, and the dog lead dangled from her wrist. They made an adorable team. "I've been thinking a lot about you, and about my interference and how that brought you here."

I was still digesting the facts myself. "I believed when I earned the grant for my building that I'd done it on my own. I thought my hard work and talent paid off, but what you told me the other night wasn't the case. I'm here because of you, and all of this is because of you."

She stopped walking and turned to look at the night sky. Her movement was slow, deliberate. "Full moon brings change." Was she honestly trying to avoid this conversation? We were both looking up at the brilliant white ball. "I'm sorry, Wil." Her voice and the way she said it sliced through me.

I wasn't expecting those words. In my experience, apologies never happened. I'd moved a dozen times in my life, and never once was there an apology. Relocation meant placing everything I owned in a plastic bag, sometimes in the middle of the night, with no words to console my sorrow or fear. I could count on one hand the people I trusted, and two of them were dead. She caught me off guard, and before I had any time to think, tears were running down my face.

I don't carry shame or embarrassment about my emotions. I'd been in and out of group therapy most of my life, and the one thing I learned was pride built walls. I was angry with Shay, disappointed, but I also trusted her in a way that shouldn't make sense. The two of us were bound not only by shared experiences in foster care but by Mama Pierce's attention and most definitively by the scars from that pocketknife and our actions in that farm field when we were teenagers.

Shay was watching me. "Please tell me that those tears mean that I haven't destroyed our friendship."

I wiped my cheeks with the cuff of my flannel shirt as I tried to sort through my thoughts. The first few weeks in this ridiculous town were replaying over and again. I scrolled through the index of experiences I'd survived. I'd spent most of my life alone because it was easier. Maybe I didn't want my life to be easy anymore. "Nothing could destroy what's between us. I wanted to be in this town more than anything. I worked very hard on that grant, and maybe I needed your help. It would have been nice to know, but here I am, and some of my dreams are already happening."

The dog barked, and we turned to look in his direction. "Dexter?" The tone of Shay's voice sounded like a question. "We should keep walking. He needs a place to do his business." I smiled. I thought they were communicating through telepathy or something cool like that. It turned out when Dexter raised his tail and barked, he needed to find some relief. "My place is the next street over. You okay if we go there? It'll be easier for him to run around."

I'd never been to her home, even though she'd been in my space many times. "It's fine. I suppose he needs to eat too."

"I'm pretty sure the fillet he's digesting right now was enough for the day." Her laugh was charming, and she reached in her pocket to find her keys. "It's the one with the orange door." The street was well lit, even without the bright glow of the moon. The rows of modest homes lined both sides, but the orange door made an impression on what was otherwise a cookie-cutter lane filled with identical single-story homes. The dog's nose sniffed at the handle and nudged the key into the lock.

"Orange is an interesting pick." I didn't hide my amusement, and her eyebrow raised with curiosity.

Dexter was half inside the door before she could open it. "It makes it easy to find in the redundancy of the neighborhood." I raised a questioning brow in disbelief. "It might also be my favorite color and reminds me to be happy when I cross the threshold."

"Does it work?"

"Most of the time." We walked inside, and Shay went through to the back of the house. Dexter was pawing at the steel kickplate on the door with his giant claws. I could see it would prevent a lifetime of damage. "Make yourself at home," she yelled back to me. I could hear her fussing over the dog, so I took the opportunity to wander.

The orange door opened into a living room big enough for a couch and a rocking chair. Behind me was a door that I had to guess was Shay's bedroom. The fieldstone fireplace with tall bookcases on either side was the real focal point. It was evident that Shay was a reader with diverse interests, but my eyes stopped on the shelves lined with references to the occult, pagan lore, and Wiccan anthologies.

There were a few pictures on the mantle. I recognized Benton in uniform with an arm around Shay. The young cadet looked innocent but still had an air of confidence. She was holding her diploma, and the scars on her hands looked brighter, new. Questions came as I wondered how she survived the brutality that left behind such horrible wounds.

The next picture was of Dexter at his graduation and an apparent recent addition to her mantle. Shay was pinning a badge on his small police vest. I saw happiness in her green eyes.

The last picture was the most interesting, and I couldn't resist holding it in my hand. I was lost in the memory of the three people, and my heart felt full. I touched the image of Mama Pierce.

"That was the only birthday celebration I ever had." I jumped at the sound of Shay's voice. "Gosh, it's so crazy. I miss her every day."

Shay and I would always have her in common. I hadn't seen Mama's face for almost ten years. It was the last time we sat together in her kitchen. When I'd heard about her death, she'd already been cremated.

"She was something," I said, wiping away my tears. "You know that I didn't know my own birthday until I lived with her. I was never in one place long enough. She did that for both of us. It's crazy to think about it now." I put the frame back in its place. "Where did you get this?"

Shay was pouring water into the stainless steel bowl on the floor. Looking up, she said, "Mama gave it to me when I went to visit her about my name change. She didn't have a lot, but she sure made up for it in love."

"She really did." I touched our faces in the frame. "She's proof that one person can change everything."

"I try to remember that every time I put on my uniform." She was standing close enough that I could feel the heat of her body. "Why don't you sit down and stay for a while. I think we have a bit more to talk about." She opened the fireplace doors and piled a mound of tinder on the cast-iron grate. The matchstick burst into flames against the stone of the mantle. She fed the sticks with kindling, building it into a crackling fire. The heat felt good, stealing away the chill from the room. "That'll burn for a while. Can I get you a drink?" She closed the screen.

"I'd love one."

She wiped her hands on the towel beside the pile of split logs. "What's your poison?"

"Surprise me," I said. Until this moment, we'd only ever shared a beer. I had no idea what kind of drink Shay might serve, so I followed her into the kitchen.

"Worried I'm gonna serve you a piña colada?"

"Something like that."

She turned toward the cabinet, holding two glasses in her hand. She rinsed them with water and placed them on the counter in front of me. "Scotch, okay?"

"Scotch is perfect. Neat."

She poured two fingers in each glass. Dexter was at the door, and she let him into the house. "Grab the drinks, and come see the back yard."

I pointed over my shoulder at the living room. "But you built a fire."

"This will only take a few minutes. That fire's good for hours." The deck in the back of the house was beautiful. Her property backed up against a thicket of shrubs and trees. It felt like being deep in the forest.

"You'd never know from the front of the house that your backyard is so beautiful."

"It's my secret oasis. The orange door isn't the only thing that reminds me to be happy. I love this place." She set her drink down on the porch railing, and her hands rested on each side of the glass. She leaned back, and I could see the release of tension from the stretch.

"This town is charming and filled with all kinds of surprises." I took a tiny sip of my drink. It was warm in my mouth, and I enjoyed the peaty flavor as I swallowed. I held the glass up in the air. "That's perfect."

She stepped away from me. Maybe it was instinct, behavior learned from repetitive academy training, to put distance between herself and conflict, but I didn't want her to see me as a threat— ever. "Wildwood, I'm going to tell you something that you might not want to hear."

I thought about the last few days. "Is it worse than demon attacks?"

She shook her head, maintaining the physical distance between us. "It's not, at least not from my perspective."

I didn't move. I just wanted to know as much as she was willing to share. "I'm listening."

"The books you saw on the shelf in my living room, they aren't just for reference." I noticed she wasn't drinking her scotch.

"I guess I'm not surprised about that. You handled yesterday's attack like a pro."

"That's not far from the truth." She picked up her drink and walked to the door. Dexter was scratching to get out, and we passed him in the opposite direction. She whispered something in Latin that I didn't understand.

I was a few steps ahead of her and looked back to ask. "What was that you just said to Dexter?"

She shook her head. "You don't miss much, do you?"

"I'm finding that I need to be on my toes around you." I sat down in front of the fire. I loved to watch the flames. "So the words you whispered?"

Shay was on the floor beside me, leaning against the couch. "If you look on the third shelf, you'll see a Latin dictionary." She pointed, and I saw the leather-bound text. "Why don't you pull it down." I listened to her instructions and handed it to her. She laughed. "It's for you."

I plopped down on the floor beside her. "I don't know Latin."

"Well, tonight, you're getting your first lesson." She slapped the cover of the book. "I said, *'vigilant ad me.'* "

I was confused. "Which means?"

She was trying to be kind, fighting back a giggle. "You're holding the Latin dictionary."

I could feel the blood rush to my cheeks. "Right." I thumbed through the pages, searching for a word that I wasn't even sure I was spelling correctly. I sat beside her, and she leaned in to help. "How do you even know this?" The book was old, and the pages felt fragile, but she didn't treat it as such. Her fingers flipped through to the back.

She hit the page with her hand. "There!" Her excitement startled me. "Latin happened accidentally," she explained. "I found this dictionary in the library at school. They were holding their annual book sale, and I loved the way the old binding looked. That's it. A few weeks later, while I was attending the police academy, I was recruited to help with the Latin translation of a file they'd found. I didn't know a stitch of Latin, but someone saw me with this book and assumed I did."

I nudged her shoulder. "You're a big faker."

She patted the open text. "Not anymore. I'm almost fluent in this nearly dead language."

I wanted to hear more. "Do you remember what was in the file?"

"It was a test." I could tell by her smile that she was excited to share the details. "I spent two days translating every word. It was a complex set of instructions that if I followed them, I'd gain access to the research office. Once I'd shared my translation with them, I was part of the demon-hunting department."

"Is that a real thing?"

"It is but, if you ask anyone about it, they'll laugh in your face. Being a ghost town is wonderful for tourism, but keeping the hounds of hell in your carriage house might be difficult to market."

"But I'm the demon blacksmith. It'll be great for business."

"You'd be surprised how wrong that statement is. Bannock didn't become a ghost town by accident." She tapped her finger on the word. "There."

"Alert?" I read it out loud.

"Well, yes, but that's just one word. The rest means to keep watch for me."

"Wait . . ." I closed the book and dropped it to the floor. "Dexter knows Latin?"

She took a sip of her drink and kicked her feet toward the fire. "Yep. He's an extraordinary animal."

"What you're saying is my favorite cop is a demon hunter with a K-9 unit that understands Latin." I didn't believe it, and I'd seen them in action. I took a sip of my drink. "So, what else?"

"Why do you think there is more?"

I turned to face her so I could read her expression. "I have a feeling that there's more to you than being great at research." For the first time since Shay returned to my life, I saw the vulnerable girl that I'd loved as a teenager. She looked fragile, and the fear in her eyes broke my heart.

Setting her drink on the floor, she pulled her knees to her chest. "I used magic to save myself after the stabbing." She took a long, slow deep breath. She rubbed the scars on her hands. "I was already deep into the study of Wicca as a religion and began doing simple spells to try and find you. Obviously, I wasn't very good, but the night Andi attacked me, I was doing something I had no business trying." Her eyes were shiny with tears, but she controlled her emotions enough to stop crying. "Her attack . . .

I've always believed that it was my fault. I should have let you go, but I wanted you back. I didn't want to be without you."

I moved to sit beside her. "I'm here now. I wish I could have stayed with you, but I'm here now." I put my arm out, and she leaned into me.

"I want you to know what I did." She was resting against me, but her arms were still wrapped around her knees. She continued talking, but I wasn't sure that she was talking to me. "I'd read a few books about location incantations. In order for them to work, you have to build up this repetitive chant of precise words. What I didn't know at the time was that it could have an effect on the people around you. She attacked me because the chant removed obstacles. It took away Andi's impulse control. She had no idea, and I didn't either. I was messing with things I didn't know enough about." Shay looked down at her hands. I touched the scars on her arms, and I waited. She pushed me away and stood to remove her long sleeves. "I can't escape the reminders, my arms, my hands . . ."

I didn't move. The only experience I had with Shay was in the past. I didn't know the adult woman standing beside me. "Look at me, Wildwood. Most people screw up, and you'd never know. Everyone gets to hide their mistakes, but I have to wear them all the time. I was so out of it. I was chanting and hallucinating so much that I didn't react to protect myself until the fourth time she stabbed me."

I didn't know what to do or how to respond to her heartbreaking confession. "Shay, I don't know what to say." She was startled by my voice. I was standing beside her, crying for both of us. I held her for the longest time without an idea of how to take away her pain.

I could feel the heat of the fireplace, and I wondered if she was cold. "Shay, please. Come sit back by the fire." She let me lead her to our place on the floor. I wrapped the flannel shirt around her shoulders. The silent acquiescence felt out of character for the strong woman I'd spent the day with. Her fingers found the scar on my palm. I didn't know how long we sat together until Dexter reminded us that we weren't alone. She pushed up from the floor and walked out of the room. Of all the events that had taken place in the last few weeks, the condition of Shay's scars hit me the hardest. She wanted me to understand what the business of her life involved. Maybe she had regrets about bringing me into her world, or perhaps she wanted me to know how important I was. I had more questions than answers, but I could tell that this was enough for tonight.

The dog came into the room before she did. Dex was off duty but still behaved like a soldier on guard. He was protecting her. I felt the vulnerability in her next question. "Would you stay?"

I shook my head at the idea that she would think I scared so easily. "I'm not going anywhere."

She wrapped the shirt around her torso. "I'm going to make some tea. Can I get you something else?" She pointed to my empty glass.

"Tea sounds good unless it's that flowery herbal crap. I just can't drink that stuff." I waved my hands to protest.

"Duly noted." She walked away with what looked like a smile.

CHAPTER V

Discovery

It was not quite 6:00 a.m. when the barking woke me from sleep. My first thought was that I didn't have a dog. My second thought was that Shay did. When I heard her voice my eyes popped open, and I realized exactly where I was and who was laying so close to my body.

"Dexter!" Her voice vibrated against my chest, and I laughed when the dog was silent.

"That's impressive." My voice sounded like gravel in a rolling can. I hardly recognized it in my own ears.

"It's all in the training." She pushed away from me, sitting up on the sofa. She snapped her fingers, and the dog was beside us. He wasn't a puppy, and I didn't think he was a pet, but he put his giant paws on the couch, sinking the cushion to lick Shay's face. "Down, buddy."

I kicked my feet to the side and sat next to her. "He always wake you up so early?" His head moved to her lap.

"It was our first night as partners in this house, remember?" She rubbed her hands together.

"Oh, right. You okay?" I hesitated to touch her.

She looked down, realizing what she was doing. "Yes, just circulation issues. Mostly from the way I was sleeping."

"Shay." I reached to hold her hand. "We need to talk about last night."

There was no hesitation or tension. She let me hold her, and it felt like a victory. "I know. There aren't enough hours in the day to tackle the damage of my past." The dog nudged at our hands. Shay rubbed his head. "Come on, Dex. Let's go outside." His eyes perked, and I realized he probably needed to do the same thing that I had to. When I came out of the bathroom, Shay was there. "Coffee?"

"That sounds exactly perfect." I took the steaming cup from her hand.

"There's cream and sugar in the kitchen, but I took a chance that you'd be a purist."

The warm ceramic in my hands felt almost as good as the first sip. "I usually only add cream to take the edge off of terrible roasting." Her eyebrow raised, and the curious look turned into a silent question. "I'm not a coffee snob. Some places over-roast, and I'm just not a fan." I took another sip. "Yours is perfect." I looked around the kitchen for a clock. "What time is it?"

"It's not quite six. I've got to run and get dressed. You'll be okay for a few minutes?"

I nodded and walked to the back porch. "I've got Dex to keep me company. Just FYI, I used the mouthwash on your bathroom sink. I left the toothbrush alone."

"Thanks for that."

I watched her walk around the corner before turning my attention to Dexter, who was running in the yard. I thought it was a nice way to start an early morning. The back porch was kind of perfect with a huge rustic swing, reminiscent of the one that Mama Pierce had. It was almost like being in the space of dreams: a slow swing, prancing dog in the grass, and a steaming hot cup of coffee. Shay didn't have a lot of flowers in her yard, which I thought was great with a new dog. I closed my eyes, thinking how romantic it would be sitting here with Shay. Dexter shifted from playful frolicking to growling and barking. Mood broken, I decided to follow the sound. He was hunched by the gate, pawing at a cardboard box with a letter on top. I took a guess that this was a recent delivery. When I reached to pick it up, the dog went wild. I dropped it like a hot potato.

"Dexter!" The sound of her voice made me stand to attention, and the dog responded the same. Shay was commanding in her full uniform. I didn't think I had an attraction to that gear, but she definitely made me stop, look, and listen. She had a cup of coffee with her, and I peeked, noticing hers had just a touch of creamer. "What do you have there?"

Dexter pawed at the package. "I have no clue, but the dog either wants it bad or he hates it terribly. I can't really tell."

Shay handed me her cup of coffee and picked up the box. Her name was written on the envelope taped to the side. "I'm pretty sure I know what this is." She didn't shake it, which went against my every impulse.

"Why doesn't that surprise me," I said, following her up to the porch.

She was smiling the way people do when they know the answer to a question but want you to squirm a little before they share it. Shay reached behind my back and took the punch dagger from the sheath. She was carrying her own, but used mine to slice the envelope from the side. I waited for flames, but they didn't come. Shay didn't seem surprised as she unfolded the paper to read it aloud.

"Hey, Kiddo. Couldn't sleep last night so I dropped this off. Tell your friend to keep notes. I'd like to know how they react after she puts them in her forge. Call me if you have questions. Benton."

She sliced the tape on the box and pulled the flaps open. There were four bundles wrapped in tattered fabric, and a small notebook tucked to the side. "Are all of these demon parts?"

She handed the punch dagger to me. "It appears that they are." She picked up two pieces and tapped them together.

I shoved the dagger back into the sheath on my hip. "Would it be inappropriate for me to ask where these came from?

She took the cup of coffee from my hands. "I'm pretty sure it would."

"So I guess I know what I'm doing today."

She put down her cup and closed the box. She handed it to me. "You're the blacksmith. I guess you need to do what you do."

I wasn't ready to leave her house or her at all. Our night together hadn't been the easiest, but it was the first unguarded glimpse of this woman I thought I knew. I finished my cup of coffee and tucked the box under my arm. "When do you start your shift?"

Shay was already wiping off the kitchen counter and packing up a few things into what I assumed was her lunchbox. Her life definitely had order. She looked at her watch. "I've got about thirty minutes. Can I walk you home?"

I hoped this meant that she wasn't ready to be apart, because that's exactly what I was feeling. "I'd love it if you would."

Shay grabbed the backpack off the chair by the door and pulled out the tiny police vest for her dog. Dexter sat motionless as Shay fastened it around him. There was a transformation, like flipping a switch. They were cops, and as beautiful as this team appeared, it was also a little bit frightening. "Dex." His ears went up, and when we walked out the door, there was an absolute absence of fear between them. After a lifetime of wondering if it was possible, I knew in this moment that I was in love with the woman in front of me. She locked the door. "Let's take a walk." I decided I would follow her anywhere.

We must have looked like quite the sight. Shay was assembled in the most perfect way. A department-issued ball cap was on her head. A perfectly pressed uniform shirt was snug over her bulletproof vest. Her duty belt was black leather, but I noticed it only made noise when she shifted her gun or taser away from her torso. Her shoes were combat style, and I thought they were impractical, but also the perfect complement to everything she was wearing. I, on the other hand, was doing a seamless walk of shame in yesterday's clothes, finger-combed hair, and barely mouthwash-rinsed teeth. I walked slower than usual because I wanted as much time with her as I could steal. I was lost in my musings when something struck me as funny. "Shay, why do you think you could cut this box open without it bursting into flames?"

"Honestly I'm not totally sure. I had a hunch, so I thought I'd give it a try."

"Kinda risky, don't you think?"

"Risk reward factor in play."

"You do that a lot, superhero?"

"Hardly ever." Her smile was dazzling. "Just in case, for future reference, there's a fire extinguisher in the cabinet under the kitchen sink."

"I'll remember that."

The walk was short, ending our trip before we had a chance to talk about our evening. My happy brain was distracted by the thought that she wanted me to come back to her kitchen. "Well this is me."

"Yes, it sure is," she said.

"Will you come by later and check on me?"

"That was my plan if it's okay?"

"Considering everything, I think it would be a great idea if you did."

Dexter was sitting at her side. He didn't react when a car horn blared across the street. "I guess that's my cue?"

I was disappointed. "I guess it is."

There was no time to react or even turn away had I wanted to. She kissed my cheek, and before I could raise a hand to touch my face, she was walking away. I fell back against the door and watched until she disappeared around the corner.

I didn't waste a minute once she was gone. I threw the box on the workshop table. Benton had labeled all four of the bundled bits with references to pages in the small notebook she'd left in the box. There was a notecard with ideas she had about what might happen based on my experience with the gatekeeper dagger. "This should be fun." I looked at the commercial fire extinguisher hanging on the wall. "And I hope I don't need to use you."

I ran my fingers through my hair, pulling it back into a loose bun. I covered it with my hat and set up the space to work. Benton had each piece listed in order from one to four, guiding me through what she thought would be least volatile. I lit the forge and waited for it to get hot.

Demon piece number one was part of a class-four creature. I didn't waste time trying to translate the Latin name into English, deciding instead to maintain Reggie's established number system. I studied the piece. I had no prior knowledge of creature anatomy, so this could have been from any part of its body. I put it inside the forge and watched it transform from what looked like bone to a chunk of demon metal. I was fascinated. Part one of demon piece one was complete. I grabbed it with my tongs and laid it on my hot-cut tool. I chopped off a piece just like I'd done on the daggers. I wanted to test each chunk on its own, but having multiple materials gave me an idea for the future. I left the project on the anvil to cool. I put demon bit number two in the forge and piece by piece worked my way through the box of parts Benton had left for me. I collected my cut-off chunks in a can, labeling them for future use. I made notes about each transformation as my fire converted them to forgeable material.

I didn't know what I expected, but I worked for hours without fearing the origins of this metal. In the big picture, this was the easiest part. I placed demon piece number one back in the forge. I grabbed an apple from the cooler. The ice had melted into a very cold tub of water. I swished my hand inside, excited about the refrigerator I'd ordered. I ate while the metal changed to golden yellow, hoping that this project wouldn't howl like the daggers, but it did. The only difference was the level of intensity, and I guessed it was because it was a class-four monster.

I didn't have a plan for the piece, and that worked to my advantage. I was so excited to figure out what this was and how it would react that I ended up making a wrist cuff. "Kinda badass." It definitely wasn't fancy, but it was effective. I hammered a raised edge all the way around, stamped it with my maker's mark, and quenched it in water. I decided the first test would check durability. Striking it with a hammer seemed easiest. I slid the cuff over my wrist and hit the finished piece with the full force of my swing. It didn't move. It didn't even scuff the surface.

"Demon bit number one is kinda like a shield. Amazons are gonna swoon." Looking at the clock on the wall, I thought about Shay. I hoped she would show up soon so we could test the strength of this new project together. I cut the supply of gas to the forge. When I was working, I shut out everything around me, but maybe I did that on purpose today. My life had just taken an unplanned turn, and I didn't know what it meant for the future I thought I had planned.

I polished the cuff against the buffing wheel until every edge showed my reflection. For a first attempt, it looked beautiful. I slid my wrist through the cuff. It was a tight fit, which meant it should be perfect for Shay.

I sat down to make notes in our *Demon to Metal* diary, admiring the mirrored edge of the cuff. It caught the light of the table lamp, reflecting what I thought was the monster who'd attacked us. I pulled the knife from my hip and pushed up from the table to take a walk through the workshop. I didn't know what I was looking for or what I would actually do if I found it. My foot kicked through the rocks and gravel, reminding me to schedule a contractor to finish the concrete for my floor.

I jumped at the sound of my favorite dog's bark. My heart was racing. I wasn't certain if it was from the spooky demon fight site or from the person at the door.

She knocked, calling my name before she walked into the workshop. "You okay over there?"

Dexter was off his lead and ran to greet me. He was sniffing the ground, tracing my footsteps back to the worktable, where my diary lay open. He barked one time and sat beside my empty chair. The dog was still on duty even though Shay wore her beautiful red hair loose around her face. She was still in uniform, but her duty belt and firearms weren't around her waist. She looked perfect, which made me very aware that I was covered in hours of forge grime. "I'm good. I just thought I saw something, and I got a bit freaked out."

"Dexter agrees with you, I think." She held a tiny treat in her hand, feeding it to the dog. As if following a silent command he lay down on the floor.

I grabbed the towel from the table and wiped my face and arms. I let my hair down and shook out the mess of the day. "Is there something we can do about that over there?" I pointed to the gravel I'd graded, the location where I'd loosed the gatekeeper demon.

"Pour some concrete, I think." Shay sat down in my chair. Dexter shifted upright and rested his head in her lap. She was rubbing the fur between his ears.

"I know that, but do we have to sprinkle some salt down or mix up a potion?"

Shay was laughing at me. I should have been insulted by the reaction, but this was another side of her that she didn't show very often. "I'm sorry. I shouldn't laugh. I'll clear the space once you've got the concrete ready. It isn't complicated, but the timing is important. Eventually I'll teach you."

"I think I need to spend some time looking at your library of books." I sat down beside her. I reached to show her my notes from the day, and she noticed the cuff on my wrist.

"That's pretty." She touched it, and I rolled my arm over so she could see the entire creation. Her finger paused over the maker's mark. "This is yours?"

"It is. It's from the material Benton gave you."

"Us. She gave it to us." Her hand didn't move from my wrist. She was thinking, and for a moment I wished I could see inside her mind. "What's it do?"

Her curiosity was almost as exciting as my own. "It's harder than anything I've worked." I turned the cuff on my wrist to pull my arm out. The metal was almost as warm as the skin of her arm. I held her hand, threading the bracer styled piece on her wrist. She didn't pull away when I touched the fading scars. "How does it feel?"

She waved her hand in the air. "It's really light." She was excited, twisting it back and forth to adjust the fit. "It looks like it should be heavy. It's not, and it feels very nice against my skin. Almost soothing."

"It's funny you'd say that. I thought the same thing. That's why I've been going through the books. I need more information about demons."

"I'm happy to teach you as much as I know. How about we exchange information, and you can start with all the details about this." She had no intention of taking the cuff off.

I explained every step I'd taken during the forging process. She was disappointed that she didn't get to hear the sound that a class-four forging made. I told her I wanted to test it now that she was here. "Take it off, and I'll show you how hard it is."

Shay leaned forward, laying her palm flat on the table. "Hit me."

I shook my head. "Oh, hell no!"

"Don't be a chicken. Hit it."

I had no intention of hitting Shay—ever. Not even to test the object she was wearing. She stood from her chair and walked to the stand beside the forge. I owned about twenty hammers, each having a specific weight and intended purpose. She took the largest one from the rack. Dexter was right beside her, and before I could make a move to stop it, the massive weight slammed against the cuff. I saw the vibration, and the room went silent.

"What the hell was that?" I saw her mouth the words.

I could tell she was speaking, but I didn't hear it at all. Was I frozen? I didn't know, but I could see the fear in Shay's eyes. She dropped the hammer before grabbing my shoulders. "Wil." She was shaking me, but I was wrapped in a silent cocoon. Her voice was muffled, and after what felt like hours, I could hear the faint sound of her voice screaming my name. I reached to grab her forearms, trying to stop her from shaking me. I blinked, but it was like closing my eyes to sleep. "Wil?"

It took more than five minutes before I could respond to her. I felt like I'd been hit with all of my hammers. "Please don't do that again." It was then that I realized Dexter was barking.

"Dexter!" She called his name, and he was quiet. "What just happened?"

"You almost killed me."

She took the cuff from her wrist and dropped it on the anvil. I could tell that the thought of hurting me wasn't something to make a joke about. I regretted my words.

"I'm sorry," Shay said. "I shouldn't have been so reckless. I got excited."

I picked up the cuff and put it back around her wrist. "This is yours, but let's take our time trying to figure out how it actually works." I opened my tiny Demon to Metal diary and made a few notes. In giant capital letters I wrote, "FREEZES EVERYONE IN THE ROOM." Shay thought it was funny, even if the notation was intended for our eyes only.

"I'm guessing that you didn't freeze when you were hammering this?" Her question was smart, and I had to stop and think if time had passed slower today.

"I didn't have any reaction aside from being able to smash the sucker without leaving a scratch or dent."

"Do you have safety equipment for your ears?" She made a motion like she was putting on headphones.

I nodded. "I don't usually wear them unless I'm teaching. The only time it's loud is when students hammer cold steel."

"You teach?"

I smiled at her, knowing exactly where this conversation would lead. "Yes, I've taught a few workshops, and I've had a student or two."

"I'll expect to get a lesson soon."

"I figured, once you saw that cuff, I'd have an apprentice and a dog to deal with."

The agreement was as good as a signed contract. "Saturday morning we start on demon chunk number two?" she asked.

"Why wait so long?" I didn't think I could put off forging for a few days.

"I was thinking you should get that corner sealed with concrete. I'm happy to help, but maybe you should focus on that?" Shay was pointing at the gravel patch of ground in the workshop. "You have a contractor in mind?"

"Yep, it's all set up. I just need to call them when I'm ready."

"I'll be on patrol tomorrow. Just give me a twenty-minute heads-up, and I'll seal the ground just before they pour."

"It sounds like you've done this before."

"I may or may not have." Her sarcastic smile was a delight. "So . . . the cuff. Put on some ear protection, and let me hit this sucker again."

I opened the cabinet and grabbed the earmuffs. They weren't special, but they were rated to silence the sound of a jackhammer. I'm sure Shay had something similar for the shooting range. She looked at me to be sure I was ready this time. The hammer dropped, and I saw the dog bark. I didn't hear a thing, but I knew the response was the same. I waited a few seconds before removing the protection.

"Anything?"

I shook my head. "Nothing at all. So if I don't hear the strike it doesn't have an effect."

"That's good to know."

We tested the cuff with a bat to simulate the use of her baton. "Anything?" she asked.

I dropped the earmuffs around my neck. "What?"

"Never mind." She turned her wrist, checking for damage.

"Maybe we should see if it's bulletproof?"

Her eyes shot open. "Maybe that's a little reckless."

"I don't mean we should shoot at it here." I held my hands up in surrender.

"Let's put that on the back burner for now." Shay's mind was going nonstop. She kept throwing ideas at me, and we kept throwing them at the cuff. "Have you tried stabbing it with the dagger you made?"

I paused on her final word, surprised that I hadn't thought to do it. "No, I didn't."

She bent down and pulled the knife and sheath from her work boot. I watched, enthusiastic about the way she wore the dagger. "That is so perfect."

She pulled the blade from the protective covering. "I thought you'd like that." She looked at me, and although it wasn't an order, I felt the command in her tone. "Cover your ears." I followed her lead, and seconds later, I watched the knife drag across the cuff.

Nothing. Not a single spark or a single flame. She repeated it a few times and then looked at me. She pointed at my ear covering. I took them off so I could hear her. "Try yours."

It didn't escape my attention that Shay was drawing a knife across an arm that was covered with knife-wound scars. "Maybe we shouldn't."

There was no hiding from the truth behind my hesitation. "Hey, it's okay. I trust you. I promise this is okay."

My approach was slow, and I watched Dexter watching me. Shay laid her hand flat on the anvil. I steadied myself to graze the cuff with a slow deliberate slice across the top. "Stop!" she yelled at me, and I jumped.

"What?"

"I think you should cover your ears." She pointed to the side of her head. "Just in case."

I followed her instruction, and when we were both ready I drew the knife across her wrist cuff. It had no effect, and I was a little disappointed. "What does that mean?"

"You're the demon expert. Why don't you tell me."

"You're the blacksmith. Aren't you supposed to know a few things about blacksmithing?"

"Not when it comes to demons." I paused, shaking my head. "Most definitely not when it comes to demons."

We decided to finish our tests for the day. She could see how tired I was, and I wanted to spend time with her that didn't involve fighting mystical creatures.

"How about some dinner?"

She nodded, and helped me collect and put away the tools. "Burger?"

I shook my head. "I was thinking maybe something at your house, in your kitchen with another glass of that amazing fifteen-year-old scotch."

"That sounds just about perfect." I locked the back door to the carriage house and turned to find her watching me. "See something you like?"

"Every time I look at you." There was no mistaking the intention behind her words. "I'd really like to thank you for this." She was holding the cuff up at me.

"First"—I took it from her and put it back on her forearm—"I want you to promise you'll keep it on."

She nodded. "And second?"

I leaned in against her until we were a breath apart. "You're welcome." I kissed her lips, feeling for the first time what I'd dreamt would always be Shay. Her hand came up to my face, and the sensation was beyond any thought or feeling I'd experienced before. It was perfect. She was perfect. This was going to be so perfect.

CHAPTER VI

Forged

What a difference a few weeks with Shay made. I was standing in my workshop, looking at the flame sputtering from the face of the forge, this beautiful red-haired woman beside me, wearing my old apron and a soot-stained hat. I'd dreamt about sharing my passion for blacksmithing with a love for so many years, and it was almost too good to be true.

The workshop was different. Shay had planted two effigies in the ground just before the thick layer of concrete pooled over them. The space where I worked looked new. The concrete was curing, and I'd drawn a small impression of my maker's mark in the corner, claiming every part as my own. Shay was finally able to come to the shop and work in the forge with me. I was distracted by her presence, but excited to show off what I could do. We were staring at monster-metal chunk number two. It was another class-four demon known as *dux mediocris*, the fairy guide. "I hate to ask this because I don't even believe it's a sentence I ever thought I'd say, but is this really a piece of a fairy?"

Shay was putting on a pair of work gloves. She didn't look up. "That piece is actually from a mass grave. I'd guess about twenty to thirty fairies are in it. They are very small."

"You're kidding me, right?"

She did look up, and her eyes said everything. "I watched a class one destroy them. It was the most horrible hate I've ever witnessed."

You should try attending a pride parade in the Bible Belt. The thought went through my brain, but it didn't leave my mouth. "So when creatures from the demon world die by fire, they turn to metal?"

"Yes, I guess they do." She shrugged. "Well . . . they did." She pointed at the pile of material.

I put the billet into the flame and watched it change from gray to golden yellow to almost bright white. It happened fast, and for a moment, I thought it was going to liquify. At this temperature, one hammer strike would cast a hot spray of flaming fairy metal everywhere. That's why we wore leathers. Mine still looked like I'd walked through hell. Demon blacksmithing left an indelible impression on the human world. I pulled the billet from the fire and set it on the anvil. I wanted to see what happened as it cooled. I wasn't ready for the whistling sound that came. I looked at Shay.

She shrugged. "I have no idea. This is all new to me."

I hesitated before my first hammer strike. The thought that this had once been more than twenty peaceful creatures was hanging heavy on my mind. The metal was red hot, and my first hit sounded like a scream. I didn't want to continue. I kept looking at Shay, and she offered no expertise. We were in this together, but clueless about what was happening.

I placed it back in the fire, but kept it below welding heat. I hammered the billet into the shape of a thick ribbon of taffy. Just like the first demon-forging experience, the longer I worked, the quieter it became.

"What are you planning to make out of this?"

"I really don't know. My thought was to heat every chunk Benton gave us and make a billet of forgeable metal. I don't know how each transforms or how much material I will have until that process is finished."

"This one looks like it got bigger, not smaller."

"I noticed that too." I was scratching my head at that same observation.

"How do you usually decide what to make?"

"That's what the sketches are for, but demon metal is special. Just look at the daggers and your bracelet. Some kind of magic happens during the forging transformation."

"So I don't need another knife or a bracelet." She was thumbing through my drawings. "Since their lives were guides in the fairy world, maybe we should make something to help us fight against the class one that murdered them."

I didn't have a suggestion and had to rely on her experience to guide us. "That works. Any ideas?"

She stopped turning the pages. "What's this?""

She'd landed on an intricate sketch of a sword. I had no idea what she was thinking. Even with the swell of material, there was hardly enough to make a knife. Forget making a sword. "It's called a Kris. It's a sword."

"Oh, I guess I didn't see it as a sword. Could you make something that's the size on the page?" She held her fingers from one end of the sketch to the other and raised them up to show a spread of ten inches. "About this big?"

I nodded and stepped closer to the drawing. "It's easy to make something smaller. What are you thinking?"

"Do you know what an athame is?"

I had limited knowledge of the tools of the Wicca world, but I'd heard the term. "Maybe."

"I think this would be perfect." She was excited. "I have the one that I used to bless the ground where our gatekeeper demon was. We should make one for you, and I can only imagine how powerful it would be."

"So we are forging an athame. Are we using this as a template?" I pointed to the sketch.

She nodded. "Yep. I like this."

I tore the page from the book and heard a tiny gasp escape from Shay's mouth. "It's okay. This is how I work. I'm a "one and done" creator. The idea moves from page to forge, and when the project is complete I burn the sketch."

"Can you explain that for me?"

"It's simple." I pinned the drawing to the cork board on the wall. I kept it in sight of the anvil so that when I needed a quick reference to the piece, all I had to do was look up. "I never forge the same project twice. Unless I'm making a pair of something, like our daggers." I picked up the fairy billet with my tongs and placed it in the forge. "My ideas are meant to be made, not manufactured. Each piece is unique." I smiled at her and tapped my chest with the tip of my tongs. "Just like me."

"You are unique in every way, my dear."

I smiled at the term of endearment. She watched me work for the next hour. I shaped the athame into a wavy ribbon about nine inches long. I hammered the demon billet, and like before, no scale or impurities were left behind. I still wasn't certain what that meant, but I'd make a note in my diary. I taught Shay how to use the tongs to move our project from the forge to the anvil. She was a natural.

She had no idea her cheek was smeared with the inevitable soot of blacksmithing, and I thought it made her more beautiful. She was learning how to taper the edge of the blade by tapping the side with her hammer. It took time, and when she finished we let it cool on the anvil. I poured her a glass of water and stepped back to admire our work.

Her cell phone rang, and I could hear the voice on the other end talking about Dexter and his visit to the groomer. I waited until she finished, but it sounded like the dog was enjoying his day off as much as we were.

She pointed to the anvil. "Can we touch it yet?" She was hovering over the project. Shay was impatient, and I understood exactly how she felt.

"If you turn your palm up." I reached out to remove her glove. "The back of your hand is very sensitive to temperature." Guiding her, our knuckles lingered an inch above the cooling metal. "Can you feel the heat?"

She nodded. "I'm guessing we should wait?"

"That would be a very good guess." I put my gloves back on. "Remember, just because it doesn't look hot, it still might be. As a rule, as soon as flame comes on, I like to behave as if everything around the forge can burn me. I really hate getting burned."

"I guess it's a good thing you're a blacksmith." She laughed, snugging her hands back into the gloves. She took a sip of water and looked at the glass. "Why don't we just cool it with water?"

"For this project, I guess we could. Would you ever use the athame as a weapon?"

She shook her head. "I might use it to cut herbs, but for the most part, I use it for blessings and just hold it in my hand." She was gesturing how she would use it, and it looked like a series of dance moves.

"When a project is this hot, cooling it too fast might cause cracks or make it brittle." I pulled out my punch dagger. "When I made these, I had no idea what was going to happen, so I quenched them in oil. I'm not sure it would have made a difference. These seem indestructible by nature."

"Okay, we have the daggers that can cut through . . ." She shrugged. "I guess just about everything."

I held her hand and drew the dagger across her bracelet. "Everything but a class-four wrist cuff."

She pulled her hand away. "Whoa."

I looked into her eyes, realizing what I'd just done. "Shit, I wasn't thinking."

A slow, calming breath puffed from her cheeks. "I'm good. You just caught me off guard. Maybe someday I'll be okay with that, but without a warning, it freaked me out."

I was an idiot. I'd spent so much of my free time around knives and stabbing weapons that using them was second nature. It was going to take time to adjust to how much Shay was adversely affected by them. "I'm such an idiot."

She was rubbing the cuff around her wrist. I knew her reaction was from the scars of her childhood. "It's okay. It's just going to take time. Being so close is kinda new to me." She could see the regret in my expression and reached to touch my face with the dirty glove. "I'll be okay, really. I promise."

"Just do me a favor and keep that thing on." I tapped the bracelet.

She held it up in front of her. "Are you kidding me? This thing looks badass."

I waved my hand over the creation on the anvil. My knuckles felt the warmth, but not the heat from earlier. I touched it and it felt cool enough to hold. "Tell me what you think about the weight."

Shay held it in her hand. It was a roughly forged blade with a blackened edge. "It feels very heavy."

"We can do a few things to fix that." I ran my finger along the end." I can cut it to make it smaller or run a groove down the center called 'a fuller.' " I drew a line down the unfinished blade with a piece of soapstone, shading the area I would change.

"Is it hard to put a fuller in?"

Her interest was exciting, and although a fuller on a wavy blade like a kris could be a challenge, I wanted to give it a try. We went back to the forge, and I taught her how to use a spring swage to make our line. This particular tool sandwiched the project so that every hammer strike would mirror the front and back of the blade. The finished athame was lighter, and Shay was pleased. I drilled small holes in the tang for pinning the handle together, and I taught her how to hammer in the maker's mark just above where the handle would be.

"Can we make it shiny like the punch daggers?"

"Yes, we can." I put the blade in the forge one final time and waited until it was fiery orange in color. I submerged it in the quenching oil, and it looked beautiful surrounded by flames. Shay stepped back to watch me work. If she wasn't enthusiastic before the quench, she was hooked on blacksmithing when I held that flaming athame in the air.

"That looks so amazing."

"I was a little worried about what would happen in the quench. Class-four demon metal seems to be safe to heat and cool." I put on heavy leather gloves. They worked well at keeping the quenched hot metal from burning my hands. The gloves were smoking, and when I laid our piece on the forge, I was happy to see that the project didn't warp. I squatted in front of the anvil to get a better view.

"What are you looking at?" She came down beside me, and I couldn't help but bump against her hip.

"I just want to make sure there's no bend in the blade."

"Does it matter if it's mostly for show?"

I stood up, holding it in my hand. I looked down the edge. "If it's for you, it has to be perfect." We weren't finished, and when I asked her about material for the handle, her only request was for a traditional ebony finish. I chose a slice of black wood and measured and cut all the parts before bonding them together with epoxy. Pins of brass fit into the predrilled holes would lock the handle together. Shay held our metal-and-wood sandwich while I clamped it together. The only thing left to do was wait for the project to dry.

"Is that it?"

"Are you getting bored with me?"

She reached to take my hand. "The opposite of that, but I might be a tiny bit impatient."

My hand squeezed around her fingers and didn't let go. I touched the scar on her palm, and traced the raised skin, but she didn't pull away. The old wound brought up feelings about her past I didn't know I had. "Is this okay?"

"Yes." Her palm was up as if welcoming my touch. "I haven't been close to anyone since Mama died. I didn't miss it until you started to touch me again."

I laid our left palms together and traced over the faded line I'd cut when we were fifteen-year-old girls. I traced it with my fingertip. "I used to look at this and wish for you to come back to me." Her adult hands were patterned with scars. The tiny pocket-knife cut that bonded us as teenagers was lost in the crisscrossing left behind by Andi's attack.

"I like to believe that having your blood as part of my own is what made me so strong," she whispered.

My shoulders came up in a shrug. "I'm not all that strong."

"Until recently, all I had was the memory. I was alone." She bumped my hip. "Neither one of us would be standing here if we weren't strong."

"I want to be here for you." I put my arm around her, locking us together in silence. I didn't know what to say, but I knew I could be with her, just two strong, broken people, forever. "You want to finish this project?"

"Just tell me what comes next."

I taught Shay how to shape the wood scales into a handle, using the belt sander. Bit by bit, she worked, contouring the material into a comfortable fit for her hand. She polished the kris to a mirrored finish. Her first project was beautiful. I had no idea I could be so happy watching her do all of the things that I loved.

"It's perfect."

I didn't have any history with the use of an athame. It was my turn to be the student. "Are you ready to show me how you use this?"

"We'll have to do that at my place," she said.

"What? No travel altar in the trunk of your car?"

She was smiling at me when she answered. "You'd be surprised what I've got in the trunk of that squad, but I walked here this morning." She was beautiful when she laughed.

The time between gluing up the handle and shaping the finished blade was enough to give all the hot surfaces in the shop time to cool. I took off my apron and hung it in the storage cabinet. The tiny mirror on the door reflected how much fun I'd had today. My cheeks were smudged, and I looked like I hadn't showered in days. I left my hair tied up, and when I turned around, Shay was watching me.

Smiling, she said, "You look wonderful."

"You could have told me my face was a mess."

"It adds to your charm, and I didn't notice it. I think it looks like you love what you do." She was trying to undo the buckle on her apron. "Can you, please?" She turned in my arms and pulled her loose hair to the side.

I noticed a scar on the back of her neck. "What's this from?" I touched it with my finger.

Her hand came up to rub the skin. "It's nothing. Just a leftover from an arrest."

It was clear that everything Shay did involved some type of risk to her body. Blacksmithing and welding could be dangerous, but as of this day, I'd never visited an emergency room because of my job. "Does it happen a lot?" My tone was harsh, and I regretted the question as soon as I'd said it.

"Not with humans." My hand pressed to the scar. She turned to look at me. "I'm going to say something to you right now. If you have a problem with the job or with the danger that comes with it, we can't be anything but friends. I care about you, and I want us to be more, but I love my job, and I can't give it up. I won't."

I had no right to ask her to be different. I barely had a right to kiss her and hold her hand. I wanted more, not less. "I wouldn't ask that of you."

"I'm not going to pretend that my job isn't difficult and that there aren't days when it's out of control, but it's my choice." She touched her hand to her chest. "It's my body, and I'll use it however I want."

I heard every word, stepping away with my arms in the air. "I got it. I just want you to know that I understand being in love with what you do, but I'm also going to worry about your safety. That's what you do when you care about someone, and I care about you."

"I care about you too." She hesitated for a second before adding, "We understand each other." She wasn't asking a question, but making a very clear statement. She put out her hand for me to shake. I felt like that fifteen-year-old girl making another pact.

I took her hand in mine, but didn't shake it. Instead, I pressed it to my chest. "When I forget that you are trained to be a cop, promise you'll remind me just like this."

"I think that sounds like a deal." She leaned in and stopped as our foreheads touched. I could feel her breath, and I closed my eyes to sketch this moment in my memories. Her lips touched my own, and I was lost in the kiss. I missed her body the moment she stepped back, opening my eyes to her brilliant smile. "If you're still able, you want to come watch me work my magick?"

I responded with a silent nod. She'd taken my breath away with one kiss. I wrapped our project in a piece of leather and tucked it in my jacket pocket. I let her guide the way, knowing nothing about the world of magick or of the Wiccan religion, but I was certain Shay would give me everything I needed.

CHAPTER VII

Magick

I decided that the walk from the carriage house to Shay's place was my new favorite path. We held hands as we talked about converting demons into weapons. The strangeness of our conversation didn't escape me. I was leaning against the front porch railing as Shay opened the door. Dexter was waiting on the other side, and I wondered why she'd left him at home all alone. "You could have brought him to the shop today."

"I thought about it." She was half in the door, pinned to the frame by sloppy wet dog kisses. "Dexter." She was laughing, and the sound made me happy.

"Someone missed you." I understood exactly how the animal felt. She patted his side, and the dog took off through the house.

"He's so excited to pee, not so much to see me." I watched her follow him to the back door, wondering if this would become our routine. Dexter hopped around the kitchen, waiting for Shay to set him free in the backyard. I leaned against the kitchen counter, waiting for her to come back into the house. There was a small box with my name on it. I was tempted to pick it up and give it a shake, but I didn't want to get caught.

She smiled at my childlike behavior. "You want to open it?"

I tried to pretend I didn't know what she was talking about, but she'd obviously noticed my curiosity. "Only if you want me to."

She pushed it across the counter and into my hand. "It's not a big deal. I just thought you'd like to have it."

I tugged the end of the ribbon and let it drop to the table. The tissue paper inside had tiny flecks of glitter that distracted me. "Just a little note, glitter makes me crazy. It gets into everything." I folded the paper back, and the frame inside brought tears to my eyes. I looked at Shay, knowing that she was the only person in the world who could understand how it felt to see the face of the woman we called mother. "She looks so beautiful." I touched the photograph of Mama Pierce, Shay, and myself. It was exactly like the one on Shay's fireplace mantle.

I didn't notice her behind me until I felt her arms around my waist. "I know how hard it is to remember everyone who has come and gone, but you were the most important people in my life."

Her thumb swiped across the glass of the frame. I wasn't sure if she was wiping her tears or mine. "I have to pinch myself sometimes," she whispered in my ear.

I put the frame on the table. "Why's that?"

"I know that the way I brought you here was . . ." She hesitated.

"Complicated?" I said.

"You're being very kind."

"I'm forgiving you, Shay." I felt her arms tighten around my waist.

"That's why I'm pinching myself. I was so worried after everything happened, that I'd be so close to having you back and then I'd screw it all up."

"I'm here now, Shay. I want to be here in Bannock, with you."

Her chin was on my shoulder. "I love you, Wildwood."

I closed my eyes. These were the words I'd dreamed of hearing. "Can you be in love with me?"

"Is there a difference?"

I was holding her hands to my chest, clinging to her warmth against my body. It was easier to confess without looking into her eyes. "I have been in love with you for as long as I can remember. I have wanted to be with you, not as friends or as pals, but as lovers." I squeezed her arms around me. I was terrified that she didn't want the same thing.

She kissed my neck, whispering into my ear, "Oh, you really are a big dummy." I was conflicted. How could she call out my insecurities while simultaneously sending shivers to all the right places? I turned in her arms. Face to face, eye to eye, everything was clear. We were going to be so good together. "I always wondered if I annoyed

you . . . back then at Mama's," she confessed. "I followed you around like a lost puppy because I just wanted to be with you."

"If you think about it, I was following you too, Shay." I kissed her.

"So here we are. Making our own decisions to be in the same place together." My eyes were closed as her hands drifted to my waist. She pulled our bodies closer, and in that moment, I let go of every fear I'd held inside. "You and I have something we need to do besides making out in my kitchen."

I didn't move. I wanted to stay in her arms. "We missed our teenage dream years. Maybe we should make out on the couch instead."

"You are quite good at helping me forget I'm a functioning adult."

I reached to touch her face. "That kinda works in my favor, don't you think?"

"Not tonight." She stepped back, running her fingers through the tangles in her hair. "Do I look as messy as I feel?"

"You look perfect to me."

"Are you going to do that all of the time?" She took a step away from me.

"Do what?" I said.

"Don't be a smart-ass. You know exactly what I mean." She held my hand and led us to the living room.

"If you're asking if I'm going to adore you all of the time, it's pretty much my plan, yes." She was my weakness. The connection was undeniable, and I was beginning to see that I would follow Shay Pierce anywhere. "Where are you taking me?"

"Did you bring the athame?" she asked.

I patted the pocket of my jacket. "Right here." I looked around the living room. "Is there a secret, sacred chamber where you work your magic?"

She held her hand to me and looked for the tiny knife. "There's nothing secret about what I believe. I'm out and proud."

I slapped the knife toward her open palm. "Me too, but not about the same things."

"You really are something." She shook her head at me and waved me toward her. "Come on."

She led me to the back of the house, into what I'd thought was a bedroom. It was beautiful, but more than my eyes could see I could feel who Shay had become. Dark walnut shelves packed full of books covered two of the walls. It was a sacred space, personal and unlike anything I'd ever entered. "When I bought this house, it was because of this room." She opened the curtain in front of the window. "The light of the sun casts beautiful colors when it passes through the stones, but the moonlight is even more stunning."

Shay was captivating in motion. I felt unworthy in her presence, watching as she opened boxes and unfolded Celtic linens. Her actions were foreign to me, as most rituals were, but her intentions held kindness and love, and I wanted to know every single detail.

"I'm not sure I'm going to be much help with this." I walked around the room. The large window looked out on the backyard, where Dexter was sleeping in the grass. I couldn't help but smile at his contentment. This house had the same effect on me. "So what are you going to show me? Is this like a church space, or what?"

She led me to a velvet-covered chair. "Sit." She pushed me into it and pressed her finger to my lips. "Be quiet." I didn't say a word.

I watched as she laid a long silk cover across the table, a delicate stitch of Celtic knots lining the edge. She adjusted the fabric until the pentacle surrounded by three moons rested in the center of the table. She opened the intricately etched, hand-carved cabinet behind her, to reveal an abundant apothecary. An endless collection of boxes and containers were hidden behind the carved oak doors. She fastened a purple robe around her shoulders, repeating Latin words I stretched to hear. She turned, placed a cup on the table, and poured water to the top.

She whispered again something I didn't hear and pursed her lips to let out a puff of air. The candle sparked with flame. I was certain my eyes shot wide open, and I gasped.

"Shh." She smiled before putting her finger to her lips, reminding me.

I had a thousand questions, but the first was how the hell she'd done that. Her movements captivated me, like a meticulously choreographed dance. She set a small candleholder on the table and placed the candle in it. She spooned tiny rocks over a smoldering bowl, filling the air with smoke and the scent of herbs and oils. I closed my eyes, trying to identify as many as I could. It was more than the sage we used to clear the carriage house after my first demon encounter. She walked around the room; only then did I notice the white line on the floor. This was her casting circle, and I felt honored to be inside it. She left the smoking bowl on the altar.

Shay unwrapped the athame, set it on a silver tray, and placed it on the table. I could feel my heart racing as our eyes met. She paused long enough to smile at me. She centered herself in front of the altar so I could watch every angle of her body.

The sound of her voice broke the silence. "Maiden, Mother, Crone, Sister, Sunlight, Moon, be here with me. Cleanse this athame with purity to return the demon energies to their creator." She held it in her hands, sprinkling something white over it. "Spirit of earth and air, bring strength and truth. Release the negative forces that formed the flesh. Make peace dwell inside this athame"—she waved the blade in front of her body—"forged from fire and called to be a force for my will. I cast away all that was evil." She waved the tiny knife through the candle flame. "As I hold this blade, it becomes my guide. For good to ward out evil" —she poured the cup of water over the athame—"now and for always to fight the wicked, it is blessed by the goddess in truth, in love, and in honor. It will move in peace and in trust and in my faith. My obeisance to truth and the boundaries of love and nature." She looked at me as she said the final words, encouraging me to repeat them. "So mote it be."

I didn't believe in a lot of things. I had very little trust in the world that raised me, but in this moment, I believed in Shay, and I definitely believed in magick. I waited for her to finish, respecting whatever goddess or higher power was present with us. I could feel the light energy of the Earth in the room, and I'd never felt so alive.

She disassembled the altar, leaving the candle to burn. "You're very good at being quiet," she whispered.

I rubbed my hands on my legs. My palms were sweaty, but it wasn't from nerves. I was excited to be in her presence, genuinely comforted by the power behind her words. "That was really beautiful, Shay."

She draped her robe over the hook in the cabinet door. "Thank you, but it's not very different from dipping fingers in water in the back of a church."

"I've never done that either."

She nodded. "It's probably better in the long run. This was a bit of a first for me too. I don't usually bless my tools."

I was confused. "Really? Why would you do it now? Is there something wrong? Was it because of me?" I rattled the questions off before she could respond to any of them.

She passed her fingertips through the flame of the burning candle. "I was taught that the work I do is a blessing. If I create with an intention for good, behave with love and stay in the light, then every tool I use to accomplish it will become sacred. Do good. Be good."

"That's really beautiful."

"It's meant to be. You taught me how important it is to pay attention to the heartbeat of the Earth. Wicca just takes it a step further."

"Will you explain why you're blessing our project?"

She picked up the athame and passed it to me. "It's all about the origin of the metal." The blade felt special, like her blessing had changed it. "Fairy energy is very strong when they are living. Every time we forge a new piece, I have to do this ritual." She grabbed the cuff around her wrist. "It was one of the first things I did after you gave this to me."

"And the punch dagger?"

"I did that too."

I couldn't hide my concern. "What about my dagger? You let me march around town with a wild and deadly dagger made from demon metal? " I unbuckled my belt and tugged the sheathed knife from it. I pinched it between my fingertips and passed it like a contaminated ticking time bomb.

She put out her hand. "I kinda had to."

I dropped it in her palm. "No, you didn't. Jeez, what if it went all wonky on me?"

Shay laid it on the tray in the center of the table. "Wildwood, what do you think I am? It's not like they are going to explode."

"I didn't say explode exactly."

"Come over here. I'm going to teach you how to do all of the things I just did." She put her cloak around my shoulders and moved to button it in front. "Are you really pouting?"

"It's not a pout so much as you just expressed how special I am, and then you let me carry around the Dagger of Doom." I picked the knife up from the table and dangled it in front of her.

"Dagger of Doom?" She shook her head at me. "Have you ever blessed or charmed a knife or blade before?" She dried off the tray my knife had been lying in.

I shook my head. "But I've also never forged demon guts either."

She blew out a long breath. "Give me the Dagger of Doom."

I flopped it in her hand, and she put it back on the altar. She held a few stones in her hand. "These are resins."

"Not smoking rocks?"

"Smoking what?"

"I saw you drop them in, and I thought you made the rocks burn."

She shook her head. "This isn't magic make-believe land, Wil. If you look in the bottom of the little bowl—it's called a censer by the way—there's a piece of charcoal. I lit it just before I dropped the resin on it. It's a combination of sage, lavender, and dragon's blood."

She hesitated before saying the last ingredient. I caught it. "You burned the blood of a dragon?" She must have thought I was that fifteen-year-old girl again because her voice made me feel like I was about to get a detention.

"Are you serious right now?"

I nodded. I believed that my new girlfriend was a sorceress, and it was freaking me out a tiny bit. "Maybe a little."

"I have so much to teach you," she said. "First, the resin is not from the blood of a dragon. It's sap from a tropical palm tree. It burns when it hits the charcoal, and there's some lavender and sage there too. The combination is for purification, clearing, and general promotion of positive energy."

"So you're not a powerful magician?"

"Definitely not." She was teasing me. "Magicians do parlor tricks. I'm a witch. I do magick."

I raised a questioning finger. "What about the candle? I saw you light that candle with a whisper and a puff of air."

"Are you sure that's what you saw?"

"Didn't I?"

She picked up the candle and held it in her hand. "Never blow the flame of a candle. We let them burn out, or we snuff them. When you blow, you cut the energy, breaking the bind." She looked at me. "I know you understand moving energy."

I nodded. "How did you light the flame?"

She didn't answer me. "Were you paying attention earlier?"

"I was." She was trying to talk around the subject.

She stood behind me, preparing to repeat the previous ritual. "Maybe one day, I'll teach you how to light a candle, but for now, I need you to focus on the blessing." I followed her movements, repeating every word. There was something intimate about sharing this magick with her. I was mesmerized as her hands touched every tool on the table. "Very good."

I passed the dagger through the flame and poured water over the top. We were finished, and although I never was truly afraid of the Dagger of Doom, I was relieved that we'd performed the ritual blessing.

She handed it to me. "Your doomless dagger."

"That's gonna stick, isn't it?"

"It is." She stepped in front of me to unclasp the cloak. "I think I'd like to kiss you right now, if that's okay." I wasn't prepared for her request. I smiled just before her lips touched mine. She clenched the cloak where it gathered at my throat, pulling me in as I pushed her back toward the table. Her hips fit against my own and wondered if it was my heart racing or hers. I wanted Shay to touch me and never stop. I was prepared to forget everything and fall head over heels for the woman in my arms.

She pulled away. "Will you stay with me tonight?"

I touched my lips, missing the softness of her own, trying to form the single word. "Yes."

Shay stepped back, taking the shelter of the cloak with her. She placed all of the tools back in the cabinet and folded the beautiful silk cloth. I took the opportunity to walk around the rest of the room. There were dozens of things I'd never seen before, and I wanted to touch every single one.

"Questions?" She leaned against the table. Her arms fell across her hips. "Just ask."

"It's not that I have questions. It's just that there's so much. The energy in this room is amazing."

"I'm pretty sure that's from everything we just did." She was standing beside me, touching her lips. "And the cleansing ritual too." She bumped my hip. "You hungry?"

"I could eat." I watched her walk away, but I didn't follow. My hand drifted over the bottles of herbs and pieces of beings that might have once been alive. The jars were marked with names I'd never read, and it excited me to know that Shay was going to teach me everything about them. My fingers traveled across books titled *A History Of Magic And Experimental Science*, *An Essay On Demonology, Ghosts and Apparitions*, and *Popular Superstitions: Book Of Ceremonial Magic*; so many texts on her wall looked older than my carriage house. I plucked a book off the shelf. The diary-style introduction to Wicca was a quick glimpse at what I didn't know about this religion. I closed it and struggled to squeeze it back on the shelf.

"You should start with that book." She was carrying a tall glass of what looked like dark beer. She held it to me and took the text from my hands. "This was one of the first books that I read. It's interesting you'd find it among all of these. She opened to the middle. "I made a lot of notes inside as I read it." She had tiny flowers, bits of twine, and fabric marking the special pages. "You might want to get a notebook because you'll have tons of questions." Shay walked away, thumbing through the pages.

I followed her to the kitchen, taking a sip of the beer as I walked. I held it up to the light, and the drink took on a red color. "This is really good. What is it?"

"The blood of my enemies."

The beer came spraying from my mouth. "What the hell? What?"

She looked up from the book. There was no humor in her tone as she held up the microbrew. She rotated the bottle's label, showing me that it was in fact the Blood of My Enemies red ale. I was horrified and delighted by the drink. "That's hilarious."

"I thought you'd enjoy it." She turned to open the refrigerator. "What would you like to eat?"

At that moment, I didn't care what we ate because I wanted her to share every detail about her life and her faith.

CHAPTER VIII

Confessions

Sharing a life with Shay Pierce, and her canine sidekick, Dexter, was never going to be dull. When I wasn't working, I was building my business and raiding the shelves of books in her home. Being together created a balance that was missing in my adult life.

I was making great progress on the second floor of the carriage house, but sharing time between her home and mine made it difficult to be in the huge empty space. My desire to make it a home of my own was fading as Shay became a priority. We spent most of our time together, but the relationship hadn't grown much beyond hand-holding, snuggles on the couch, and kisses. We didn't talk about intimacy, but I was sure that we both had wounds from childhood preventing us from becoming lovers.

I thought about her all of the time, and if she wasn't a complete professional, I'd be battling Dexter to become her daytime companion. I was hooked, and hooked deep.

The kitchen space of the loft took a few days to complete, and I could cook a meal if we ever stayed that late. The cabinets didn't have doors, but the look was growing on me. Today's adventure in construction was all about filling the bathtub for the first test run. The floor was the original hardwood with a thick layer of polyurethane protectant. It was beautiful, and my plan was on track to maintain the architectural integrity of the building, but if I was honest, I really wanted to soak in the tub. I'd been dreaming of it since I found the clunky thing in the scrapyard. The porcelain wasn't perfect, but every ding and scratch gave it character.

The last step in achieving my goal was fitting the faucet fixture. The chrome pieces were new, and I researched the purchase, keeping true to the early-nineteenth-century style. It was an investment, but when I tightened the crisscross knobs in place, it looked like it had always been in the room. I turned the handle, releasing a sputtering combination of water and air. It sprayed my face, and I was done. The walls were half-finished with plaster and lath, but I didn't care. I was getting into this tub.

I didn't have fancy fluffy towels, but it didn't matter. The real luxury was the result of my hard work. I held my hand over the steaming water, and I could tell it was going to be hot, but that wouldn't last. I leaned to touch a toe, and it felt perfect as I plunged my foot inside.

At twenty-eight, this wasn't my first soak in a tub, but it was my first carriage-house luxury-bath moment, and I wished I had a candle or two to make the experience a dream come to life. I was impatient as I fell back against the pitch of the tub, and I was done. My arms slipped out of the water to rest on the rounded porcelain edge. I closed my eyes, disappearing into the thought that this might be my new favorite place.

I didn't know how long I'd been soaking, but the water had cooled enough to wake me with a chill. I felt something against my hand, and for a moment, I forgot everything and thought of Shay. I heard the bark, and my eyes opened to a beautiful dog face followed by panting and whining for more pats on the head. Dexter was in my bathroom, which meant that Shay wasn't too far away.

I sat forward, reaching for the towel. I pulled the chain from the tub and watched the water spin through the tiny drain hole. "Hi, Dexter." I shuffled the hair between his ears. "Where's your partner?" Water was dripping on the floor, but I didn't care. I was looking for Shay. I didn't have fuzzy slippers or a fluffy robe. I put my wet feet into my work boots, tightened the towel, and went in search of my Shay.

She was standing in my kitchen, half out of the refrigerator, looking adorable in part of her uniform. "Breaking and entering is a crime, copper."

She froze and raised her hands in the air. Her back was turned, but I could imagine her brilliant smile. "I promise I didn't break anything when I entered." She reached for the key I'd given her and dangled it from a finger. "And this came with an open invitation." She turned around when I didn't respond. Her silent gawk was all I needed. She scanned the length of my body, and every pause in her glance felt like hands burning against my skin. "That's an outfit, sweetheart."

I realized that it was difficult to look tough in an old towel and unlaced steel-toe boots. "When did you get here?" I walked to greet her.

"I've only been here for a few minutes."

I saw the pan of chicken and chopped potatoes on the stove, and the salad on the counter. "What's a few? I swear you've got no sense of time." I stood in front of her.

"Maybe a half hour." She shrugged it off. Her arms came around my body. "Dexter got impatient and wanted to see you." The dog was nowhere in sight.

"Dexter?"

"That's my story, and I'm sticking to it," she said.

My hands were on her cheeks. I kissed her, surrendering my body to the strength of her arms. "It's very convincing."

She picked me up and turned us around so she could watch the food on the stove. "Are you hungry?"

I stepped out of her arms and leaned in to smell the sizzling pan. "I am now."

"I've got a couple of minutes left on this." She floated the pan over the flame, tossing the contents with a flip of her wrist.

"You're a chef too?" I watched her cook. "A girl could fall in love with you, superhero."

"I'm only interested in one." She turned her attention back to me. "You going to eat wearing that?" She pointed at me with the spatula in her hand.

"What, not formal enough for you?" I pretended to be wearing a gown, drawing my hands down the neatly tucked towel.

"Oh, it's fine, but I'm not sure I can focus if that's all you're wearing."

"Maybe, Officer Pierce, I don't want you to be so focused." I stepped closer to her.

"Wildwood." I heard fear in the way she said my name. "It's . . ."

I put my hand over her heart. "It's okay. I'm teasing."

"I just . . ."

"It's okay. I promise." I touched my forehead to hers. "Please, it's okay."

She held her arms around me. "I—"

"Just keep cooking our dinner, hero. I'll be right back." The laces of my boots slapped my naked calves as I walked back into the bathroom. There was water on the floor, and Dexter was right beside me. "Damn it," I whispered to the dog. "I need to be more patient." I was talking to myself as I toweled off and got dressed. I wasn't planning to work for the rest of the night, so a loose T-shirt and pair of jeans would do the trick. By the time I made it out to the kitchen, Shay had places set and was filling Dexter's bowl with food.

We didn't live together, but we did keep small bits of ourselves in each other's homes. Sharing space made sense, and it also made life easier. The dog abandoned me for the dish of kibble. "Go, you. I'm sure mine's going to be so much better."

"It will be for sure." Shay put the food down. "Come sit, you very loud dog whisperer."

"Ha, that's funny." I took a seat at the table.

We ate in silence. I wasn't sure how to start a conversation about the obvious miscommunication in the kitchen. I was grateful for the courage that Shay always managed to muster.

She put her fork on her plate. "I know it's been frustrating for you. That I've been frustrating you."

"I'd never do anything to hurt you or make you feel uncomfortable."

She looked at me from across the table. "I know that." Her sigh was a whisper. "I want to be with you, Wil, but I'm not sure I'll ever be able to stop reacting with fear and shame every time you look at me like that."

"I'm probably one of the only people in your life who understands what it means to survive a childhood like ours." I paused to make sure she could see in my eyes exactly what my words meant. "I know what it's like to fear the light and the darkness in a room. I get that no one is ever just handed your trust." She was shaking her head at me. "I also know that there is nothing that can change the scars on your body or how you got them." Tears were flowing down her cheeks.

"Being touched is one of the most difficult things for me to deal with." She took a sip of her water and wiped her tears on a napkin. "Being a cop . . . No one questions separation and distance. Self-preservation is part of the job. Keeping physical distance makes sense. It's socially acceptable to never touch anyone all day long." I could see the pain in her eyes, and I waited for the rest of her story. "I've made a very safe life for myself, and honestly, I was fine with it."

I raised a questioning eyebrow at her. "You have a safe life fighting demons in a ghost town?"

"That's not what I meant." She shook her head, managing a tiny smile. "I mean I was socially safe in a town where I work with mostly straight guys who see me as an equal. No chance of fraternization, and everyone keeps their hands where they belong."

"But you brought me here, Shay." I pushed my plate away. She was a confusing woman.

"I know I did." Her hands went to her hair in frustration. "When I heard your name suddenly I wanted answers. I didn't care about the rest." She pulled out the elastic tie, releasing her hair to fall around her face. I wondered if she realized that move didn't relax me at all.

"I would never pretend or diminish anything you've been through, and I'm here right now, expecting nothing more than holding you."

She interrupted. "But—"

"I'm human." I was honest. "As much as I've dreamed of being with you, holding hands won't always be enough."

"I know that too." She stood from the table and carried her plate to the sink. "What if I'm never ready?"

It suddenly occurred to me the possibility that Shay hadn't ever been with anyone, and my heart was breaking. I walked to her side and leaned against the sink. "Have you ever?"

"Ever?"

She really was the most extraordinary woman I'd ever met. "Been loved. Been touched by a lover?"

"No." She shook her head and her hands came up to cover her weeping eyes. "It's not that I don't want sex. I've just prevented the opportunities."

"Stop. It's okay to be afraid, Shay." I leaned in closer, careful not to touch her. I waited. I knew in my heart that I always would.

"I wished for you to come back to me. I full on dreamed that you would come back to me and this stupid broken part of who I am would be different."

"Have you ever talked to someone about this?"

"You mean professionally?" Her hands gripped the edge of the sink. "I've been talking about it with a counselor for years. Most of our conversations were about what-ifs." She stepped away from me. "I don't even understand myself. I want you. I've always wanted you, but it was like a dream that kept me here, that helped me stay alive."

"What do you mean?" I was confused, and the more she talked, the more I didn't understand.

"I just never believed that if you came back into my life that it would ever be more than a beer at the bar, and I could go home at night and just dream about being with you."

I waved at her to come closer. I waited. I hoped. When she took that cautious step toward me, I held out my hand. "You don't have to dream anymore." The tears were breaking my heart.

"Maybe I really am just broken." Her hand touched mine.

"Maybe we all are." Her skin was cold. "So what?" We stood in the kitchen, leaning against the sink. Her hand was in mine, and nothing else seemed to matter.

"Can I ask you something?" I was startled as her voice broke the silence.

"You can ask me anything."

She squeezed my hand and let it go. "Have you had many relationships?"

I nodded. "A few."

She bit her lower lip. "Hmm."

"What's that mean?" I asked.

"Nothing, really. I just don't want to be the reason you're unhappy."

I held her hand and directed her to look in my eyes. "If I'm unhappy I promise I'll tell you, but right now, I'm here with you because I want to be here."

"We're in your house, Wil."

"That's not what I meant, and you know it."

"I know, but my heart hurts. The way you stand here and say everything I've dreamed you would and I still can't let go of my past."

"Do you want me, Shay?"

"More than I thought possible, but . . ."

I pressed a finger to her lips. "There's no 'but.' After all these years, after everything, I'm not going anywhere just because you're scared."

She released a calming breath. "Okay."

I'm no saint. There was truth in every word, but I wanted to touch her body more than I wanted anything or anyone in my life, but I also loved her enough to wait. Our dinner was abandoned half-finished, but I'd lost my appetite.

"The bathtub looks amazing." She tried to change the subject.

"That bathtub is a dream." I reached for her hand. "You should use it every chance you get."

"I just might," she said.

"Can I ask you a question, Shay?"

She started cleaning up the food on the stove. "I guess it's your turn, yes."

"It's very personal."

She turned around to look at me. "Just ask. After all of this, if I'm not comfortable, I'll tell you."

"I want to ask, but I'm not sure I have a right to." I stood beside her at the kitchen sink.

She shook her head. "I've never been with anyone if that's what you're wondering, but it's not because of a bad experience or sexual violence." Her hands dropped in the soapy water. "After Andi attacked me, I just got lost in protecting myself. People scared me."

I didn't know what to do with the information or the level of honesty she shared. "But I don't?"

She shook her head. "You never have. In fact, I talked to you all of the time." She handed me a soapy plate, and I rinsed as she explained.

"You talked to me?" I started to dry the dishes and put them in the cabinet. "How so?"

"Of all the places I lived, you and Mama Pierce have always been the memories that felt like home." She rinsed her hands and took my towel to dry off. "I couldn't see you every day like I wished, but I could tell you everything and hope somehow that you'd know."

"I wished for you too."

"The way they moved us around, it shouldn't be like that." She walked back to the table and finished her drink. "The foster care system is still bullshit."

"Yes, I know." I reached across the table to hold her hand. "So you became a cop to make it easier for others?"

"It seemed like the perfect fit for so many reasons."

"How about we get out of here and take Dexter for a walk?" At the sound of his name, the dog moved to stand between us.

"It looks like my canine partner agrees with my human partner." She squeezed my arm.

"Are you asking me to be your partner?" I stopped, surprised by the comment.

She dropped my hand and walked toward the stairs. Without hesitation, she looked over her shoulder. "If you can handle it, yes, I am." I followed her. She lingered on the bottom step, and I bumped against the length of her body. She turned, grabbed my hips, and spun us around to the landing. "I am asking you to be with me. I know I'm not easy sometimes, but you mean everything to me."

"Yes." I smiled at her and nodded.

She kissed me. "That was pretty easy."

I put my arms around her hips. "You don't even know the half of it."

Dexter's barking interrupted the conversation. It was his voice breaking the calm, telling the two of us that something wasn't right. Shay was stripped down to her uniform basics, in a V-neck undershirt and work pants. Her first instinct was to move in front of me and reach for the gun on her hip. Her duty belt wasn't around her waist. "Shit, my gear is outside in the squad." She pushed me up the stairs. "Go back." I hesitated. "Now, Wil. GO!" There was no question in her voice as we backstepped to the second floor.

The dog was getting louder and advanced toward the workshop. Shay pushed me until we were against the doorframe leading to the bedroom. She opened the closet and dragged a storage trunk across the floor.

"What the hell is that?" I asked, slapping my hand on the giant box.

"It's a present for you, but I'm going to have to open it." She looked up at me, at the same time noticing the fear in my eyes. "Hey, it's okay. I've got you." She gave my hand a calming squeeze. Her reaction to the moment was so fluid that I had to concentrate to follow her. A belt came out of the box, followed by a baton and a taser. Her spare gun was pulled from the pancake holster, and she was ready to go. Dexter's barking went silent. "Do . . . Not . . . Move!"

I watched her turn and run from the room. I sat frozen on the floor. Here we were again. Since Shay had returned to my life, I felt vulnerable, and I didn't like it at all. The seconds ticked away like hours. The building was silent behind the pounding of my nervous heartbeat.

"Wildwood!" she yelled up the stairs. "Grab the green bag from that box and come here." I rifled through the container until I found the compact duffel.

I dropped to the first floor, taking two stairs at a time. Shay held up her hand to stop me and grabbed the canvas bag. "Put your hands out." I followed her orders, and she slapped the taser handle into my palms. "Any movement, pull that trigger." It was a command, not a request, and I nodded my understanding. She removed a small box made of wood. I followed the taser leads stretched out in front of us, and although the room was dark, I could see that the probes were buried in the chest of something huge and distinctly inhuman.

She ran toward the demon, reciting words in Latin. I watched her sprinkle white powder on the ground, creating a circle around the creature. Dexter was silent but on guard. It was like a scene from a movie, but it was happening right in front of me. "Where's the Dagger of Doom?"

I shifted the taser into one hand and pulled my knife out with the other. "Here."

"Slide it to me." My eyes never left Shay or the tethered demon behind her. I launched the dagger across the floor. Shay grabbed it, and in one motion cut the leads to the taser.

Sparks flew around her hand as two tiny flaming wires slapped back at me. One caught the corner of my cheek. "Ow, damn."

She turned to look at me. "You okay?"

I touched my face, and a tiny drop of blood rested on my fingertip. "Just a scratch."

Dexter's barking was louder and more ferocious. Shay stood at the edge of her circle. "Come here, Wil. I need your help."

I was still holding the taser, feeling as stunned as the monster on the ground in front of us. "What is it?"

She grasped my hand, feeling the bulk of the taser first. She tossed it on the ground. "Take this." I was holding my punch dagger. She positioned me beside her. "I want you to repeat every word I say. Every word!" Her voice was calm but commanding, leaving no space for deviation.

She was speaking Latin, and I guessed, in that moment, I was also. I mimicked the sounds just like a parrot until I understood and remembered two—*Huic ostiarius*. Gatekeeper. This was my demon, my dagger's parent. Shay was silent. There was a flame that seemed to burst from nowhere, and I watched as Shay dripped liquid from a glass jar. She followed the outside of the circle, and the demon lay frozen inside. "*Hirundo*!" Her voice was loud and startled me. The concrete opened, and the demon melted into the solid ground.

"What the hell!" I looked into the flame-lit workshop. "What the actual hell, Shay?"

She was digging around in the bag. She held up four candles. "Come help me, please, and I'll explain." Shay was looking at her watch, but it wasn't to check the time. She found the north point of the circle and planted the green candle. "Your gatekeeper needs to be locked behind his own damn gate." She whispered something in Latin.

"In English would be helpful for the non-Latin speakers."

She looked up at me. "Right, I'm teaching."

"Do you have to use Latin?"

She shook her head and continued to move clockwise around the white ring. "I don't, really. It's just a habit." She placed the yellow candle in the location most east. "Air, in form and collective manifestation, join my circle." She continued, stepping around the edge, lighting the flame as she placed each candle. "I'm calling on the elements of nature," she shared, setting the red candle on the ground. "Fire, gift of the sun, tempered to bring forth balance, join my circle." She didn't stop moving or explaining what she was doing. "I'm asking in all directions for their presence." She lit the blue candle at the western point. "Gift from the sky to the seas, bring forth nourishment from the streams. Water, join my circle." She took the green candle out of my hands and lit it. "From the caverns below to the mountains above, Earth, join my circle."

"Are you casting a sacred circle in the middle of my workshop?"

"I am." She put out her hand. "Dagger of Doom, please." I saw the mischief in her eyes that matched the smile on her face.

I placed it in her palm. "You're never going to stop calling it that, are you?"

"Why would I? It's the perfect name." She crossed the white line of her circle and placed the purple candle in the center. "Shh, this is the important part." She lit the last candle.

"Should you step inside like that?"

"Shh!" The sound of her purposeful whisper was sexy as hell. "Purity of our sacred flames." She turned in the circle, rotating the dagger to each candle point. "Goddess and divine beings, bless this sacred ring. Pour goodness over the shadow. Cast out evil to balance and make whole. Gaia, connect us in spirit. We ask for safety and protection. Close this space, this gateway. Give this place to goodness and peace in the light." She looked at me, guiding me with her eyes to repeat her final words. "So mote it be." She passed the dagger to me in the palms of her hands. I realized it was acting as her athame. She stepped in the opposite direction she'd lit the candles and walked out of the circle.

"Now what?" I pointed at the white ring on the floor.

"We let the candles burn." She opened the wooden box and returned all of her tools to the canvas bag. "Now we talk about what just happened in here, but we have one more thing to do." She patted Dexter on the head and whispered, *"Vigilant ad me."*

"Keep watch." I whispered the translation, as I put my dagger back in the sheath.

"Nicely done." Shay was impressed.

I pulled my hand across the damp tangles in my hair. "I think I need a drink before we do anything else."

She picked up the bag. "I'll take a beer, maybe two." I followed her to the kitchen and then to the bedroom. She sat down on the floor in front of the trunk. I handed her a beer before taking a long sip of my own. I'm not sure alcohol was the best choice.

I sat beside her, looking inside the box. "I had no idea this is what you brought over."

"I knew we'd need it." She laid the contents on the floor and closed the trunk.

"Is this an altar?"

She was moving through the tools with purpose. "Very good. You get a gold star."

I clapped for myself. "The purple cloth is a giveaway."

"I knew your gatekeeper was coming back."

I rested my hand over the tools. "What do you mean?"

"Before you poured the concrete, I put two figures in the ground." She was setting up the altar just as she had at her home, but stopped when my hand covered hers. She looked into my eyes. "One was meant to call it back."

I swallowed hard. "Call it back?" I had spoken louder than I'd meant to.

"Yes. Call it back to the broken circle."

"Don't you think you should have told me that?"

She didn't move. "It didn't matter."

"What do you mean it didn't matter? What if you hadn't been here?"

"That's impossible."

"What do you mean 'impossible'?"

"That's what the second figure was for. I bound it to me."

"Are you crazy?" I pushed away from the makeshift altar and stumbled back toward the bedroom door.

She grabbed my hand, stopping me from walking out. "We were never in danger."

"How could you possibly know that?" I pulled away from her, but she held tight.

"Just listen to me." She walked us back into the room. "The circle protected us."

"There wasn't a circle. I dug it up."

"Take a deep breath, please."

Her voice was calm, and it pissed me off. "I don't want to take a deep breath." I crossed my arms in front of me. "I want to know what the hell is going on."

"Shh, for just one minute so I can finish this binding."

I stayed back and watched her. She followed the same order, setting the surface with candles and herbs. "Dagger of Doom, please." She held out her hand.

"Why don't you use your own?"

She stood in front of me. "If I had it in here, I would. My gear is in the car, and there isn't time." She held out her hand.

I saw the scars, and they reminded me that she was on my side, but I still wasn't pleased with anything happening in this room. "Fine. Here." I slapped it in her hand, and she walked back. She was kneeling in front of the display, placing the dagger in the center. She whispered something in Latin, and it irritated me even more. "In English, please!" My tone was harsh and impatient.

She looked up. "Yes, my mistake." Smoke twirled in front of her face. "Mother, Maiden, Crone"—she clapped her palms together—"Wisdom of the ages"—she held her palms above the dagger—"unbind them through this." She sifted white powder over the candle and the dagger. "Remove the flame." She looked up at me as if to request my participation. "So mote it be." I repeated her words, and she closed her eyes. The candle went out as if responding to Shay's command. Everything about her was unexpected. When it came to magick and fighting demons, I was getting tired of being lost and in the dark. I waited. She sat quiet for the longest time. "Will you help me, please?"

"I thought I just did." I was coarse and unapologetic.

"Wildwood, it's important for you to lay your hands on everything. You unearthed it, so you must help me bind it to the gate."

I followed each request until we finished packing the tools back inside the trunk. I was still angry, but mostly because of my fear of the unknown. "Are we finished?"

"Yes."

"Am I safe now?"

"Yes."

I didn't say another word. I stood from the floor and turned to leave the room. I threw my beer at the sink and walked down the stairs. I stood in front of the giant white ring burned into the workshop floor. Dexter was lying in the circle, and I knelt to touch the ground. I didn't understand how, but the ring seemed permanently etched in the concrete. Shay was standing behind me.

"I know you have a lot of questions. I'll do my best to answer all of them."

"Let's keep it simple," I interrupted.

Her hands were shoved in her pockets. "Go ahead."

"Did you know all of this was going to happen?"

"Yes." She didn't deny it. "I knew the demon was coming back. It had to. Something or someone not of this world bound it to the carriage house. I was protecting you."

"Here's the thing. I don't want you to do that anymore."

"Protect you?"

"No, do magick for me without me."

She shook her head and walked around to the opposite side of the circle. She knelt down. The flame of the candles burned bright enough for our eyes to meet. "I'm not going to agree to that. I can't. There are things you don't understand."

"Then as much as I want you, us, I need to take a step back." I stood to walk away.

Shay held up a hand as if to keep me from moving. "Just like that?" She wanted me to stop.

My heart was racing, and my response was louder than I intended. "Just exactly like that! You have to respect my right to choose."

"Wait." She pushed off the ground and stumbled backward. Her hands slapped against the floor, and she was covered in dirt. "Perfect." She dusted her palms over her pants. "Just perfect."

"You okay?" I wasn't heartless. I took no pleasure in watching her fall.

"I'm just perfect. Didn't you hear?"

"I also saw it."

"Damn it, Wildwood. You have to listen to me."

I crossed my arms but didn't move. "What could you possibly say that changes what happened here today?"

"I'm not a monster." She was standing beside me. "If anything—and I mean anything—happened to you after what we've been through, I could never forgive myself."

"You sent a damn demon to my workshop."

"No, I didn't."

I was confused. "Maybe you should explain."

"That's what I've been trying to do." She put out a hand. "Will you come upstairs so we can sit down?"

I shook my head. "I think I'd rather stay right here. It's closer to the door."

"Are you kicking me out?"

"I guess it depends on your next few words."

"You understand that, when you dug up the binding circle, you broke the tether holding that monster in the earth."

"Yes, I do understand that part."

I could see the desperation in her actions and hear the fear in her voice. "If I was going to keep you safe, I had to put it back. That thing is a gatekeeper, and without it, this building would be a colossal magnet for goddess knows what."

"You know I'm not even upset about that." Shay was confused. "You really don't get it, do you?"

"I'm trying to," she said.

I held up a single finger. "I'm going to say this only one time." I didn't touch her, but I was in her personal space. "You don't get to make decisions for me, and you don't get to do any magic for me without me."

"Do you know what you're asking?"

"I'm pretty sure I'm asking you to treat me like an equal."

Shay turned and walked away. She didn't say another word until she came down the stairs, carrying the trunk. She set it down in front of me. "Open this."

"Why?"

"Just open the damn trunk!"

I lifted the top.

"Set up the altar."

I took out every piece I remembered. I closed the lid and placed them where they belonged. Shay took my dagger from the sheath on my belt and placed it in the center.

"Open that, and light the black candle." She pointed to the hand-carved box beside me. I did everything she asked without question.

"Now tell me how you're going to protect us from a class-two demon?"

I couldn't answer her question, because I didn't know. I wasn't the expert on magick, and I had no idea how many different demons even existed. "I don't know how to do that."

"That's the thing. You don't have to, because I do."

"I think you're missing the point, Shay." I didn't like the way she turned this conversation around. She was making a clear point about why she did the spell. What she was failing to see was how it made me feel that she did the spell.

"Yes, I think we both are." She sat down in front of the altar, blowing out a frustrated sigh. "Will you please just tell me how to fix this?"

I sat beside her, with my back to the trunk. "I was scared. I'm scared of this." I slapped the altar with the back of my hand. "I'm scared of what I don't know." My hands fell into my lap. "And I'm scared of what's happening between us because of it."

She reached to hold my hand. "You have to believe that I know what I'm doing. None of this will work if you don't trust me."

"What if you get hurt?" There it was, an honest confession of my truest fear.

She didn't shy away. Shay tucked a hair away from my cheek and touched the cut left behind from the taser's lead wire. "I probably will, just like you did tonight."

I swatted her hand away. "It's a scratch."

"They usually are. It comes with the job."

"What if I don't want to be a demon fighter?"

"Then I'll be one for the both of us."

"But from now on, you'll tell me when there's a fight, and you'll ask me if you need help?"

"I promise." She made an *x* over her chest. "I cross my heart."

I turned around to look at the tools on the trunk. "Why did I light a black candle?"

"You want the truth?"

I slapped the side of her leg. "Those are fighting words."

She held up her hands in surrender. "Black candles are used to release negative energy, and they are also meant to bring enlightened thinking."

"Did you just magick me with my own magick?"

She pushed up from the floor, shaking her head. "No, you just opened our minds and released all of the fear. If you give me a chance, I can teach you how to do all of this."

"If you promise to include me in the decision making. You have to let me choose."

She collected everything from the altar. "Hold this for me. I want to do one more thing."

I was interested enough to do exactly what she asked. She placed the tools inside the trunk and closed the top. She held out her hand and helped me from the floor, but she didn't let me go. "Give me the candle." She took it and placed it in the center of the circle. "It's important to keep this circle closed, Wil." I nodded in agreement. "Every day for the next week, we should light one and leave it until it burns out."

"Do I need to worry about the gatekeeper coming back?"

"Only if that concrete crumbles." She stopped. "You trust the contractor?"

"Gosh, I hope so."

"Me too." We were standing in front of the trunk. "So does this stay or go?"

"Are we talking about you or the trunk?" I bent down to take a handle.

She did the same, and we lifted it together. "Both, I guess."

"You can stay, but only if this partnership is even." I walked toward the staircase. "Should we just keep it in the office?"

"For now it might be a great idea." We set it in the corner beside my table. The plans for demon forging were laid out. Shay's fingers drifted over the sketches. "Is this the next experiment?"

I picked up the piece of paper. "Yes. I thought I'd make a candleholder out of the class two."

"That's interesting. Why?"

"Everything I read suggests that this monster spits a stream of blue fire. I thought it would be ironic if it held a flame for us."

Shay seemed to agree with my idea. "What are the chances I can get that beer?"

"I'd say your chances are excellent if you'll come back up to the apartment."

The weight of the evening hit me as I opened the refrigerator. "I know it's not much of a bedroom, but will you stay with me tonight?"

"I'm not sure that's a good idea."

"Does that mean we haven't come to an agreement about this relationship?" I handed her a fresh drink.

"Look at me. I'm a damn mess." She set the drink on the table. "I've got an early morning. I want to take a shower and sleep in a bed."

"You don't like the mattress on the floor." She shook her head. I sat across from her at the table. After so many weeks the furniture was still sparse. "I'll see what I can do to fix that."

"Do you feel safe, Wildwood?" She was peeling the label from her bottle.

I shook my head. "I'm not sure that I do."

"I'm sorry that the way I chose to protect you was scary."

"I am too."

"Do you think it would have been easier if I told you?"

"I guess we'll never know."

"Can you forgive me for that?"

"I think I can, but if you want me to trust you, you've got to trust me too."

"I understand that."

I leaned in to hold her hand. "You don't have to do everything alone . . . Not anymore. I don't know what I have to do to convince you that I'm not going anywhere."

"I've never had to consider how my life would impact someone else's."

"It's amazing how you can surround yourself with a room full of friends and still feel unseen and alone."

She stood up. "I see you. I'll always see you, and I want to be with you." She finished her drink and turned to leave.

"I want that too, Shay." I put out a hand to hold her wrist. I didn't want her to leave.

"Can you be patient with me while I figure out how to let you in?" she asked. I nodded. I could see the exhaustion in her features as she looked into my eyes. "I'll come by to check on you during my shift tomorrow." She kissed the top of my head, and she was gone. I heard her feet on the stairs and the sound of

Dexter going out the door. The apartment felt empty without them.

CHAPTER IX

Fire

I couldn't sleep for many reasons, but the buzzing loudest in my brain was the way Shay walked out of my apartment. I didn't want her to leave, but I'd made it impossible for her to stay. We shared the same experience of surviving foster care, but that's where our paths moved in different directions. I poured my pain into creating as an artist and blacksmith, and she poured hers into the world of demons and magick. I wondered if it was possible for us to find solid common ground.

I worked through the night, losing all sense of time, building a frame for my bed. I didn't need much more than the mattress on the floor. When I was tired I could sleep in any position, but if we were going to share our space, mine needed to include room for Shay. I only meant to rest my head for a few minutes, but I'd fallen asleep in the office, leaning over the sketches under my arms. The sound of knocking on the workshop door woke me. The clock read 11:00 a.m., and I was sure it wasn't Shay.

I stopped to check my reflection in the mirror, and it was obvious I'd been awake all night. I pulled my hair back into a loose bun and answered the door.

"Hello, I'm looking for Wildwood Blackstone."

The gap was wide enough for her to see me from head to toe. "I guess you found her," I answered.

"You?" She pointed at me. "You're not what I expected." She pushed past me before I could move out of the way.

"I get that a lot." We stood inside the workshop. "How can I help you?"

"My name is Andrea Peters." She held a hand out for me to shake. "I work for the City of Bannock." She was neat in her tailored skirt with a loose-fitting blouse under her coat. She was older than me, but not by much. We shook hands, and she continued, "I was talking to Regina Benton about your project."

"My project? I'm sorry, I'm not sure what you mean."

"Ms. Benton shared some information about a certain talent you have. I'm interested in hearing more details." She wandered around my workspace, dragging her finger across the top of the anvil. She was trying to be discreet, but I could tell she came to satisfy her curiosity, picking up my tools as if she'd never touched one in her life.

I followed her into my office. "I don't mean to be rude, but I'm not comfortable discussing my 'talents' with you." I used air quotes around the word talents to emphasize my point. "I don't even know who you are." She reached into her purse and handed me a business card. I read it out loud. "Andrea Peters, assistant to the mayor of Bannock." I dropped it on my desk. "I'm not going to talk with you, Ms. Peters. I'd like to talk to Ms. Benton first."

"I see." Andrea was an intriguing woman, and I got the impression that she didn't hear the word *no* very often.

"If you'd like, maybe we can schedule a time to meet next week." I gave her my business card. "Can I reach you at the mayor's office?" I walked her toward the exit. I didn't like the way she resisted leaving.

"You can," she responded. Making it clear that she thought she was in charge.

I opened the door and caught a glimpse of the Bannock police squad pulling around the side. I didn't feel threatened by this woman, but not knowing her intentions was more than a little unsettling. Dexter was at the door long before Shay. I rubbed his head between the ears, and he barked a greeting. "Hey, buddy. Where's your partner?" He sat in front of me, wearing his service vest. I didn't miss that he was using his body to put space between us and the assistant mayor.

Shay stopped in front of her squad car, noticing my visitor. I couldn't tell until she was closer that she was talking on her cellphone. She ended the call and approached my guest.

"Peters." Shay said the last name never taking her eyes from me.

Andrea didn't look at Shay. "Pierce."

Their greeting seeped with forced civility, and I wanted to know the story behind it. Shay walked right up to me and kissed my cheek. "Hello." The maneuver felt like she was staking her claim, and in this moment, I didn't mind. Dexter barked at us, looking for equal attention, so I dropped down and hugged him. Shay was standing between us, physically placing herself as my protector.

"Do you need some help, Andrea?"

"Ms. Blackstone and I were just discussing her blacksmithing skills."

"Were you, really?" Shay asked. I took a moment to watch my girlfriend. She was solid, unwavering in her questions, and when she wasn't pleased with the answers she escorted Andrea away from the building.

"Perhaps you'll convince her to speak with me?" Andrea urged.

"Perhaps." They were standing beside the only other car parked in front of the carriage house. Shay opened the driver's side door and closed it after Andrea was inside. The entire scene was curious, and I wasn't sure why Shay intervened. She stood on the sidewalk until the assistant mayor drove away. Her expression was professional, and her body language relayed complete control of the situation. She was sexy as hell.

When she was close enough to hear me, I asked. "Should I be worried?"

She put her hand on my shoulder and pushed me inside the building. "She's a real piece of work. Don't tell her anything until we talk to Benton."

"You going to tell me what that's all about?"

Shay took her hat off and wiped her forehead on her sleeve. "Benton called me at the station. She sent me over to see you."

"So this is a business call?" I didn't hide my disappointment.

She wobbled her hand. "I'd say it's fifty-fifty." She leaned against the frame of the door. "I don't greet everyone with a kiss."

I smiled. "Well . . . *Officer* Pierce," I said, "what can I do for you?"

"First you can tell me if we're okay."

I took the hat from her hand and brushed the stray red hair off her forehead. I kissed her cheek and popped the hat on my head. Her eyes were closed as I stepped away, and she touched her face where my kiss had landed. "I guess that's an answer."

"You don't have to guess . . . It is." I walked toward the office. Dexter was already lying in the corner, on a blanket folded into a makeshift dog bed. "Tell me what's going on with the assistant mayor?" She wasn't following me.

"Did Andrea come inside the building?" Shay was standing in front of the circle on the workshop floor.

"Yes, she did."

"Damn it!" Shay yelled at the empty space. "That woman is so infuriating."

I wasn't happy being in the dark about who Andrea Peters was, and I was equally curious to know about the relationship between them. "I'm guessing there's a story here."

"That'd be a good guess." She looked up and finally noticed the hat on my head. "My hat looks good on you." She tapped the brim with her finger.

"Thanks." I tugged it back into place.

Shay turned on the faucet in the corner to fill a bowl of water for Dexter. "Assistant Mayor Peters is the worst representative for this town. What makes it more complicated is that she knows about me and demons, and now I guess she knows about you." She set the bowl down on the floor.

"What does she know about me?"

"Wait, can we pause for a minute?" She made a little *T* with her hands to call time-out.

"It depends."

"Don't worry. I'm going to tell you everything, but I need to know that you and I are really okay."

I took her into the office and pushed her to sit in my chair. "We will be okay as long as you tell me the truth and you see me as your partner. I know that being equal in this . . ."—I prodded the pile of demon metal—"is going to take time, but no more secrets."

She grabbed my hips and pulled me closer. "No more secrets, but sometimes there will be need-to-know situations."

I pushed against her shoulders to look into her eyes. "What does that mean?"

She pulled me into her lap. "It means being a cop takes first priority, and if it's confidential, I'll tell you whatever won't get me in trouble."

"That sounds fair."

"Good." She turned the office chair to look at the drawings and notes on my desk. I wrapped an arm around her shoulder and watched her scan the desktop. "Did Andrea come in here?"

"Yes, why? What's wrong?"

"Did she use her phone? Did she take any pictures?"

"Not that I remember."

"Grab the diary. Don't close the page. I need to know exactly what she saw."

I passed the book to her along with the few sketches from the table. "Is this bad?"

Shay nodded. "She came here fishing for information, and I'd say she found some." She scanned the notes. "Damn, I thought we'd have more time to understand all of this before meeting with the higher-ups."

I raised my hand, waving it in front of her. "I think this might be a good time for you to explain what's actually going on in here." I tapped the side of Shay's head. "Your brain is moving a mile a minute."

She tried to stand up, but I gripped the back of the chair to hold her in place. I needed her to stay. "You understand that mixing human and demon encounters can get very tricky to maintain. The mayor knows everything. His discretion is vital to keeping a town like Bannock from returning to empty 'ghost' status." She made tiny quotation marks with her fingers. "I don't work alone as a police officer, and I don't work alone as a demon officer."

"Demon officer?" I shook my head at the silliness of the name.

"It's not an official title, but the idea is about the same here in Bannock."

"And Andrea?"

"She thinks demons would put this town on the map." Shay tossed the book on the table. "We have to guess that she knows about the daggers and maybe the wrist cuff. She also had to see those billets." She stood up, lifting me with her. "I think we need to finish more projects and forge more of this material."

I liked the idea. "You will never have to ask me twice to blacksmith." My feet dropped to the floor, but she didn't let me go. I turned in her arms to face the top of my workspace. I spread all of the sketches out.

"We should try to forge another billet before meeting with Benton. That way, we have more to share."

"*We* should, huh?" I asked.

"I'd like to help."

"I'd like it if you would. Plus, it's always good to have the best-trained demon officer on hand." I hesitated. "Just in case."

She agreed. "That's very smart." She squeezed her arms to hug me.

"What time are you finished working today?" I asked as I sat down on the edge of the desktop.

She looked at her watch and at the dog in the corner. "Dex and I will be here around four. That'll give me time to go home and change out of my uniform."

I sighed. "You should bring some stuff over. Keep it here, I mean." I turned so we were face to face and she was standing between my legs.

"Should I?"

"I know I don't have much for closets, but I'll put up a bar in the bedroom and make some space in the bathroom for you."

She smiled and leaned in to kiss me. Her lips were soft, and I lost myself in the sensation of her against my skin. The real magic was happening between us, and I didn't want it to stop. She pulled my body closer to hers. She was strong, and as she lifted me I felt her gun and taser press against my hips.

"I'll swing by the house now so that Dex and I can come right here from work."

I held the sides of her face, looking into beautiful green eyes. "That's perfect."

She kissed me one more time, pressing her hand to the back of my head. Her hat slipped off, and before I could open my eyes, she stepped away. She tugged her BPD hat back in place. "I should go." With a snap of her fingers, the dog was beside her. "I'll see you in a little bit."

My fingers touched my lips, and I smiled. She was gone, and I was left to figure out how to sort through all of the people in this town that I didn't know but who managed to know everything about me. I needed more, and my hope was that Shay could help me.

I spent the next few hours building a rack for Shay to hang her uniform. I wanted my space to feel like she belonged in it. I had no intention of compromising who I was to be with her, but if we could navigate the complexity of her job and my own, we might just be amazing together.

Before I realized, the afternoon disappeared and Shay was knocking on the door. She was still in uniform, and I rewarded her with a kiss for following the plan. We were standing in the kitchen when I asked her how the rest of her day had gone.

"I got a hand slap for escorting Andrea out of the carriage house." She didn't even try to hide her satisfied smile.

"Really?"

"Yep. It was worth it though." She looped her hat on the hook by the door. "I'm going to change. You ready to play?"

"Am I ever?" She followed me to the bedroom.

"You've been busy." She set her bag on the bed. "You built all of this?"

I nodded. "I did the bed frame last night. I couldn't sleep."

She turned to look at me. "I'm sorry, Wil."

"It's okay. We have an understanding. That's what matters."

"Yes, we do." I could sense her apprehension.

"I'm going to let you change. Does Dexter need anything?"

She started unbuttoning her uniform. "Just water. I'll feed him when we eat later."

I kissed her and walked out. She was here in my space, and it felt like a home. It didn't take long for the dog to settle in on the workshop floor. I wasn't certain if it was weird that he liked to lie in the permanent circle etched in the concrete.

Shay was wearing a tattered Grateful Dead T-shirt and faded jeans. Her hair was pulled back and covered with a tie-dyed bandana. She was going to be the most amazing partner.

"So where do we start?"

The plan was to forge a candleholder from the class-two demon billet. I'd sketched a few designs, and we chose one that required the least amount of material. Drawing out the metal took extra time, and the howling sound that it made startled Shay until it subsided. I was able to create eighteen inches of demon steel. I chopped off three inches, just like before, and added it to the can in the corner.

"What are you planning to do with the cutoff pieces?"

I shrugged my shoulders. "I've got an idea, but I want to surprise you." I continued to fold the project back and forth like a ribbon, creating the base for the candle.

"Oh, I love surprises."

"I hope you mean that." The last eight inches swooped in a curve to create the handle. We added the maker's mark, completing the beautiful project. Cleaning around the forge, I noticed my partner was very pleased with herself.

"I can't believe we made something so beautiful." The candleholder was cooling on the anvil.

I picked it up with the tongs to wire brush any scale left behind. The workspace was clean, and I didn't understand how a demon creature's billet of metal wouldn't produce impurities. "The lack of scale is unnerving."

"What do you mean?"

"I think I explained that forging and hammering creates tiny flakes of metal. Not one of the demon projects has produced a single bit." I picked up a rusty piece of steel. I waited for it to get hot and struck it with my hammer. There was scale when I moved it away. "See, that's what should happen. I don't get it."

"Do you think it's important?"

"Don't you?" I wiped my face with my sleeve. "Until we know enough I think everything is important."

"You'll have to let me know what else looks different. I don't know anything about blacksmithing."

"Not yet, but you will."

"You ready to test this? See what it does?"

I checked to see if the candleholder was hot. Once it cooled I carried it to the office. "I've got some old beeswax candles in here."

"I've got some in the tool kit." She turned to go upstairs.

"These are fine. I just need to get the right box." I moved the trays in my cabinet until I found what I was looking for. "This should be perfect." The recycled wax was used to seal finished projects, and it fit well in the base of our candleholder.

"It looks amazing."

"We can use this on the altar at your house, if you'd like." I picked it up and carried it back to the forge. "You want to do the honors?" I handed her the box of matches.

"I've got an idea." She held out her hand. "Dagger of Doom, please."

I smiled. "You have no idea how much I regret calling it that." I lifted my work apron and drew the knife from the sheath.

She took it from my hand. "I think it's perfect." Shay set the candleholder on top of the anvil. She picked up a piece of scrap metal and arced the blade against it, throwing sparks at the wick. The flame was bright blue. "I was hoping for something more exciting."

I hooked my finger through the arched loop and picked it up by the handle. "The blue is pretty cool." I walked around the workshop. "It's easy to carry. I like it." She was silent. I twisted in her direction. "Shay?"

"Look at the wall."

The flame flickered as I turned around. "Holy crap, what in the hell is that?"

The wall was smeared with the outline of ancient runes lit by the blue light of the flame. "It's like magic luminol," she said.

"Isn't that for blood spatter?" I cringed at the thought of ancient drawings written in blood on my workshop wall. I continued my walk around the room. When I turned to talk to her, she was gone.

"It is." Her voice faded as she entered my office. "I've never used it, but the department has it in the crime-scene kit." Shay returned carrying my sketchbook and a pencil. She started copying the characters on the wall. "Come back over here for a second, and light this up again." In cop mode she was adorable. The blue flame was solid, illuminating the entire space.

"It's a little creepy to see this on the wall in here."

"I don't know. It's interesting, and I wonder what this building was really built to hold." Her paper looked like artwork you'd see in an early-childhood classroom. "We're going to need to run to my house and get a book on translating Nordic runes."

She dropped the sketchbook on the desk, and I set the candle and Dagger of Doom beside it. "You want to walk with me, or stay here?"

I looked down at my apron keeping my clothes clean enough to go outside. "I'm up for a walk."

Shay waved her hand over the flame. It kept a steady glow. She pressed the dagger to the top of the wick. The fire kept burning. "That's funny."

The expression on her face didn't match the tone in her voice. "You don't really think that it is, do you?

"Do you have a candle snuffer?"

I shook my head. "I've never used one. I had no idea I shouldn't just blow them out."

"Bring the candle and the sketchbook."

I unbuckled my apron and hung it in the cabinet. I held the candle while Shay hooked Dexter to his leash. "What are you thinking, Shay?"

"I'm thinking you made daggers that can't be broken. A wrist cuff that freezes an attacker." She was counting them on her fingers. "We've got an athame that we haven't even tried to figure out, and now a candleholder that burns an endless flame."

Dexter was trotting beside her, excited to be outside. The night air felt cool against my skin. "Forging demons is an adventure," I said.

"Sweetheart, that is the understatement of the year."

I stopped. "*Sweetheart*, huh?"

She smiled. "I think it fits."

I didn't know what else to say. I would be her sweetheart for the rest of my life if she let me. We walked the few blocks separating her place from my own. Dexter knew the way home, and when we turned the corner onto Shay's street, he was ready to run. "Dexter." His butt hit the sidewalk, and he waited for her command. She unclipped the lead and waved a hand to let him loose. "*Ire!*" She yelled the instruction, and the dog took off at full speed.

"What did you say to him?"

"*Ire.* It means go." She put out her hand for me to hold.

"Do you trust him to run like that?" I asked.

We watched him race to the front porch. "I trust his trainer."

"Didn't you train him?"

She laughed as she pulled the keys from her pocket. Dexter nudged the key with his nose as Shay unlocked the door. "I did." He was through the house and waiting by the back door before we were inside. "Why don't you look on the shelf by the fireplace for the book on Nordic runes? I'm going to let the wild beast out."

I set the candleholder on the table and looked through the shelves. I was still trying to understand how so many books were written about Wicca and the pagan faith.

"Did you find it?"

I was startled by her voice. "There's about a thousand books here. I might need a librarian."

Her fingers traveled over the shelf, and in a few seconds, she had the text she wanted. "The translation might take me a few minutes. Why don't you work on extinguishing the flame?"

She spread the books and sketches on the kitchen table while I spent the next twenty minutes trying to find a way to extinguish the demon candlestick. Shay laughed when I put it in the sink, running a steady stream of water over the entire project. After a few seconds, the flame flickered out.

Shay interrupted the silence with a random thought. "Water. That's interesting."

I looked up at her. "Yes, who would have thought to extinguish a flame with water?"

"What now?" She scribbled a few words before looking at me. "What did you say?"

I held up the water-soaked candleholder. "I just thought it was funny that you thought using water was interesting."

She tapped the notes in front of her. "That's not what I meant. The runes on the wall are a spell, and they reference the power of the four elements."

I didn't have a clue what she was talking about. "Is that good or bad?"

"It's very good. That's exactly how I locked your gatekeeper right where he belongs." She was tapping on the page with her pencil. "I'd like to go back to the carriage house and look at the wall again."

I was excited to be part of the research. "Whatever you need to do."

"There's a symbol here that I don't think I drew right. I need to look at it again." She piled the books and notes into her backpack. She disappeared into the altar room and returned with a small stash of herbs, and jars filled with mysterious liquids. "Will you grab the box from the closet behind you?"

Shay had a heavy-duty, wheeled toolkit in the kitchen closet that I'd assumed was packed with power tools. I opened the cover, and nothing was inside. "It's empty."

"We're about to fill it, unless you want to carry all of this down the streets of Bannock." I shook my head, and I packed each of her magic tools inside. "You're bringing the athame?"

"I've got a couple of ideas that I want to sort out. It'll be easier to have it with us."

"Are you expecting any demons to show up?"

"You'll learn soon enough, Wil. I always expect demons in Bannock."

CHAPTER X

Marked

Shay was right about dragging the toolbox across town. It was heavy with herbs, rocks, books, and magick tools I couldn't identify. In a final last-minute scurry through her room, she'd tossed in some clothes and her robe. Once we returned to the carriage house, we set up the sawhorse table, and she spread all of the research on top of it. I lit the candle, and Shay directed me as I held it up to the walls. She took pictures with her phone, printing them as we continued to document every rune. Although her sketches were accurate, they didn't capture the details hidden by the reflection of the blue flame.

"Just like we thought."

"Remind me what we were thinking again." I never wanted to be inside someone's brain as much as I wanted to be inside of hers.

She waved me over. "The runic text is very clear. It's definitely a spell to cast a gatekeeper back." Her finger traveled over the photographs from her phone. "But this one, the way it's written, it isn't like what's in my books."

I looked at the picture and back up at the wall. I carried the candle, walking to stand in the middle of the workshop. "Where's that image at? Where in the room?"

"The south wall." She pointed and followed me to the spot. She held the candle to compare the picture to the small rune in front of us.

"Don't you recognize it, Shay?"

She shook her head. "I don't."

I grabbed her wrist and rolled it until my mark was visible. "Look." I held the cuff I made over the photograph. "They're almost identical."

"*Your* maker's mark?" Shay dropped the candle to the floor. "How the hell does your maker's mark appear in demon blood on the wall of this carriage house?"

I shook my head. "I have no idea." I picked up the candle. I watched as my girlfriend's forehead contorted, her brilliant mind sorting through all of the information. She was back at the table, assembling the tools I'd forged from the billets of demons.

"Give me the Dagger of Doom, please," Shay asked. I placed it beside her knife and the wrist cuff. The athame was added to the collection. "How long have you used that mark on your work?"

"I started stamping all of my projects with this one when I moved to Bannock." I opened the cabinet holding my tools. "When I got the contract for the carriage house, I wanted to incorporate the new location. I took my original and added a few distinct lines." I was digging through my chisels and punches.

"Here's the one I used before the move. It's a medieval hammer." I held the two side by side. "For the new mark, I added the half-moons around the outside edge." I used the tip of her pencil to point out the changes. "And the five lines are meant to represent the wheel of a carriage."

"How is this even possible?" She wasn't asking me the question, just throwing it out to the universe. "Do you see that it makes a pentacle?"

I compared the sketches. "I didn't until just now."

"I don't believe in coincidences." Shay walked away. "I need to think." She collected the notes and a few books, and carried them up the stairs to the kitchen table. Dexter was lying on the floor, but didn't move when she sat down.

I had no idea how to help, but I could keep her energy up. "Can I feed you?"

Her pen paused on the page as she looked at me. "I could eat, but I'd really like to take a shower."

I set the pan on the stove. "You can use the tub. It's got a new sprayer. It isn't great, but it'll knock the dirt off."

She dropped the pen in the crack of the book, marking her page. "As long as the water is hot."

"That won't be a problem." I gave her a towel from the basket. "I just washed these; they're line dried, so I'm sorry about the scratchiness."

She kissed my cheek. "I can handle scratchy." I could see the fatigue in her eyes.

"Take your time. I'll dig around in here and see what I can cook up."

The food inside my refrigerator looked bleak. I had a few eggs and a half loaf of bread. I could make scrambled-egg sandwiches or French toast, but I had no idea if Shay would eat either. I knocked on the door to ask her thoughts. When I heard a mumbled reply, I peeked my head inside.

Shay's shirt was half over her head, and I wasn't planning to interrupt her undressing, but I did. Her abdomen was exposed, but I could only see the scars just under the elastic of her bra. I never should have opened the door, and my gasp was loud enough to freeze Shay with her arms half over her head.

I didn't move. I couldn't. So I watched Shay's panic as she hurried to wrap her torso with the crumpled shirt. I couldn't pretend I didn't see the marks left behind by her attacker. "Oh, Shay." I was frozen in the doorway. "What did she do to you?"

"Please, Wil. Please don't." Her fisted hands punched through the sleeves as she pulled the shirt down to cover her scars. She stumbled over the pants and shoes tossed on the floor.

"Oh, Shay, I didn't . . . I didn't mean to just come in." I wasn't certain what my apology was for, if it was meant to comfort this accidental break in her privacy or the knife wound scars she kept hidden.

Shay leaned against the giant tub, frantic to pull on her pants. The zipper caught against the seam, and I noticed the trembling of her normally steady hands. "I need to go." She didn't bother to button her pants.

It was clear to me that these scars were the unexplained barriers I'd been fighting to break through. I stood in the doorway, preventing her from leaving. "Please don't be afraid of me." I held my hands to her shoulders. "Please." Her head was down, but I could see her cheeks were streaked with the stain of tears. "Please don't run."

She stopped, using the frame of the door to catch her balance. Her eyes met mine, and I saw that fragile girl who'd suffered unspeakable violence. I opened my arms. She hesitated before falling against me. "I'm here, oh love. I'm here. It's okay." Her body was shaking from the intensity of her crying. "Shh, it's okay. I've got you."

I repeated it over and over as we stood in the doorway. I could feel her hands clenching the back of my shirt. Shay was the strongest woman, but the pain of trauma never really went away. A wet dog nose pushed in between us; Dexter must have sensed her pain. We didn't respond to him, and the force of his concern increased. He pushed against us until Shay reacted.

"Dexter, down." Her voice staggered through the sound of tears. I reached for the towel on the hanger so she could wipe her face, and she used it as an opportunity to put space between us. "Wow, this isn't me. I didn't mean to fall apart."

Officer Shay Pierce spent her waking moments being strong, hiding the pain and vulnerability left behind after the childhood attack. I didn't know. There was no way I could have. "Are all of the scars from Andi?"

The look in her eyes was the only answer I needed. "Yes, they are."

"I had no idea."

"No, you wouldn't." She looked down at her hands. "Most people think that these are the real scars."

I held her hands in mine. I tugged them so she would look into my eyes. "I'm sorry, Shay." I kissed her right palm and then her left. I rested them against my heart and kissed her lips. I felt her body tremble. "I'm sorry I wasn't there to protect you."

She let her forehead rest against my own, tears still falling from her hazy eyes. "No one was there for me after. I just covered them, and that's what I've been doing ever since."

I wiped away her tears with the pads of my thumbs. "Come with me." I held her by the hands, leading us to the bedroom. I could see the fear in her eyes. "Trust me. I'm not going to let you fall." We sat together at the edge of my bed. "Do you want to talk about it?"

She looked down at our joined hands. "Since you've come back into my life, I've done everything I can to avoid talking about this."

"Would you believe me if I said I understand why?"

"I think so." She was staring at the doorway, where Dexter had spread his body to protect her. "It's easier with him." She nodded at the dog. "He's seen me naked and never once made a sound or noticed."

"And I did." There was nothing I could say that would undo my reaction to seeing the scars on her chest. "I'm—"

She touched my lips to stop the next word. "Please don't say you are sorry." She wiped her eyes with the fabric of her shirt. "It hurts more. It reminds me that I've kept so many secrets."

"I don't know what to do, Shay."

Tears collected in the corner of her eyes. I wasn't prepared for the vulnerability in her next words. "Tell me you can love me even with all of the scars."

The desperate look on her face cut me to the core. "I can love you any way that you'll let me, scars and all."

There was no way to know if she believed me or if this trust was strong enough to get us through. She climbed up the blanket and rested her head on my pillow. I could feel the exhaustion as I pulled back the blanket to cover us. She didn't say another word. I held her through the tears, until she fell asleep. I'd never hated my childhood as much as I did that night. I despised the people who'd abandoned her, but there was little I could do to erase her past, even though I was determined to try.

My body was as restless as my mind. What could I do to fix her pain? How could I make it better? It wasn't possible, and when I surrendered to that truth, I wanted to run. Looking at who she'd become made me feel weak and undeserving. How could I ever live up to the woman beside me? I shifted and turned until I couldn't stay in bed any longer.

Just after midnight, I left her alone to sleep. Dexter followed me down the hall, and I decided a late-night walk might help us. I'd never had a dog of my own, and Dex was becoming the perfect first. We wandered through Bannock for more than an hour, until I heard the sound of my own stomach. We managed to stop in front of Slammed and decided to visit with our new best resource for information, Reggie Benton.

Dexter made fans and friends everywhere he went. At Slammed he was a star, but tonight, the bar was empty. Benton met us at the door and was happy for the late-night company. "How'd you manage to separate that guy from Shay?" She led us to a table.

"Shay's sleeping, and he needed a walk."

"Rough night?" Her hands rested on the back of the chair.

"More than I can share right now."

"What can I get you?"

"How about a beer and answers to a couple of questions?" I grabbed a handful of pretzels from the bowl on the table.

"I'll be right back."

Dexter was sitting on the floor beside me, and I felt a little guilty leaving Shay on her own. Benton set a beer on the table for me and sat down. "So what kind of answers are you looking for?"

I twisted the bar napkin. "Tell me about Andrea Peters." I took another handful of pretzels.

"Shay mentioned Andrea stopped in for a visit. I'll give you the same warning I gave to Shay. You need to steer clear of Andrea until you finish our project and give your creations a test run."

"Is she that big of a deal?" I popped a pretzel in my mouth.

"I wouldn't say that so much as she's a big maker of noise, and right now, I want to keep her as quiet as possible."

"What's her angle?"

"The most I can tell you is that she wants what you have."

The ambiguity of her answers was frustrating. "Are we talking about the carriage house, or someone else?" I looked up at the clock behind the bar, noticing how late it was.

Her short laugh said it all. "It's not a secret that the two of them dated."

"Dated? Really?" This was an interesting piece of information that Shay hadn't shared. I didn't know Benton well enough to ask for details. I checked the clock again.

"Why don't you finish that beer and head back to Shay? Come by tomorrow, and you can pick my brain a little bit more."

"That obvious, huh?"

She walked away. "It sure is. The beer is on me." Reggie waved a hand to say goodbye. "See you tomorrow."

I finished my drink, noticing how quiet it was in the bar. I hadn't spent a lot of time socializing without Shay, and it felt like I'd abandoned her. It was just after 1:00 a.m. when Dexter ran up the stairs. He wasn't quiet, but it didn't matter, because Shay was in the kitchen, making scrambled eggs and toast. Her hair was wet, and she was wearing a pair of my sweatpants and an old T-shirt. In my clothes, in my space, she was beautiful.

"You been up long?" I questioned my decision to leave her alone.

She didn't turn around. "About thirty minutes." She stirred the eggs in the pan. "I woke up, and you were gone. When I didn't find Dex, I figured you'd taken him out."

"He needed a walk."

"How about you?"

"I wanted to let you sleep."

She spooned the eggs onto a slice of toast. "I hope scrambled eggs are okay."

"That's what I was going to ask when I walked in on you. I was coming to see if you wanted eggs or French toast."

"Oh." She stopped cooking and turned to look at me. Her eyes were red around the edges and swollen from tears. She set the plates on the table. "Eggs. I'll always eat eggs." She pulled out a chair for me. "Eat something."

I grabbed her hand. "I didn't mean to leave you alone."

"It's alright. I needed the shower and some time to think."

We ate in silence, and when I finished, I stood at the sink to wash the dishes. Shay folded the rug on the floor for Dexter.

"I'm going to go back to bed. Is that okay?" she asked.

"Yes." I started drying the dishes. "I'll be right there. Just let me clean up." I put the plates in the cupboard and wiped the table. I knew I was avoiding walking into the bedroom, hesitating as I approached the doorway. I knocked, waiting for a response.

"It's your bedroom."

I peeked around the door. "I know that, but I didn't want to do anything . . ."

"Get it the damn bed, Wil." She could order me to bed like that for the rest of my life. I stood beside her. "Are you a right-side sleeper?"

She sat up against the headboard. "Not generally. I just climbed in."

I pulled back the bedspread where she was laying. "Good. Scoot over because this is going to be my side." The sheets were warm where she'd been. "Thanks for warming me up too."

"Are you going to be the boss in here all the time?" she asked.

"I hope you're kidding because you telling me what to do is a major turn-on."

"Good. Now get over here and help me warm this side too." She opened her arms, and my head fell against her shoulder. I was at a loss from there. I didn't know where to put my hands, so I tucked one under my head and the other on my hip.

She was quiet for the longest time, and I was content listening to the drum of her heartbeat.

"Are you afraid to touch me?"

I propped my head so I could see her. "I'm afraid of a lot of things, but mostly I never want to see that look on your face ever again." She closed her eyes, and I could tell she was trying to put her feelings into words.

"Do you ever tell people that you were a foster kid?"

I rolled onto my back and looked up at the cracks in the old ceiling. "I don't really talk to anyone about my past. After Mama died, most of my connections went with her."

"We're cut from the same cloth, you and I."

My heart was racing. Her voice, laying on our backs side by side, I was fifteen again, and I wanted to kiss her. I felt her hand in mine, and I lifted it to my lips. "I've tried very hard to leave behind all of the things that I couldn't control, Shay." I traced the deep scar on her palm.

"That's not as easy for me," she whispered.

"I know. I wish you'd told me."

She was quiet again, and as annoying as it was, when she broke the silence, her words didn't disappoint me. "There are only a few people who know what my body looks like." Her voice broke as her chest raised with a deep breath, building courage to share her truth. "It changes people, knowing that I was nearly stabbed to death. There are expectations and encouraging words and distance." I listened as she explained the tragic reasons for the wall she'd built to protect her body and her soul. "I didn't want you to see me differently. I didn't want you to see me as less."

I needed to undo the damage I caused. I was trying to decide the truth behind how I was feeling. I didn't want to say anything that would keep us apart. I was silent for so long. Shay squeezed my hand. "Are you sleeping?"

"No. I'm sorry. I was just thinking about you and your body." I didn't mean it the way it sounded, and although her tiny laugh did ease the tension, I wanted her to know.

"Does it make you feel different?"

"Yes, it does." Her head was shaking against my pillow. I turned to see tears rolling from her eyes. "Shay." I sat up beside her and reached to wipe her cheek with my thumb. "I feel different because you've become this wonderful person. You turned that attack into something powerful and empowering. You don't have to hide yourself from me or from anyone else." I gathered her in my arms and held her through the tears. "I'm here for you. Whatever you want from me, I'm here."

"I want to stop feeling this way."

It was well past 2:00 a.m. when she relaxed in my arms. I was comfortable holding her and realized that although we weren't making love, this was the most intimate I'd ever been with a man or a woman. I wanted to feel this way forever. Shay rolled on her side, and I held on close behind her. My arm draped over her hip, and I was aware that I hesitated before touching her scars. Everything was going to take time.

I heard the alarm on her watch at the same time I felt her body move to silence it, 5:30 a.m. came too fast. In the short hours we spent sleeping, my arm had drifted around her. The hem of her shirt had fallen away, revealing her abdomen, and my hand was pressed against the warmth of her skin. We realized at the same time where I was touching her. I tried to pull away, but she held me closer. "Please don't."

My body tensed. "What?"

"Stay. Just stay." I did exactly as she asked. "I've wanted this more than I knew. Just be with me a little longer."

I held her until the second alarm went off. Shay turned in my arms. "I don't want to leave," she said.

"I'm glad you feel that way. I'm not going anywhere."

"But I have to." It didn't take long for her to react to the last alarm on her wrist. "I've got thirty minutes to be at the station." Her feet were touching the floor.

"You need food?"

She shook her head. "I'll grab something on the way." She took her clothes into the bathroom, and when she returned, she looked like the commanding woman the world knew. I realized what a privilege it was to be with the unguarded side of Shay Pierce. "You just gonna lay there and watch me get dressed?" She pulled her hair into a tight ponytail.

"I've got nowhere to be." I pretended to look at the watch I wasn't wearing.

"That's cute."

I stayed on the bed, entertained by the systematic routine as she dressed. "I'm intrigued by the way you gear up."

"Gear up?"

"I'm watching you, the delicate woman who was curled up in my arms, transform into a powerful public official." The sound of the heavy-duty velcro brought Dexter to the bedroom door. "Is that a Pavlovian response."

She fluffed the fur between his ears. "I guess so. He knows it's time to get to work." She dropped the vest over her head and cinched the velcro strap around her torso.

I jumped up before she covered it with her uniform shirt and knocked my knuckles against the center plate. "Take care of that heart under there."

"Bulletproof and ready to roll." She held my hand against the vest. "Thank you for last night."

"I think I should be apologizing instead of being thanked."

"I needed you to know."

"I'm glad that I do."

She stepped away to put on her shirt. It was unbelievable to me that watching a woman fasten ten buttons could be so sexy. She carried her duty belt to the kitchen and hung it over the chair. Dexter was waiting to gear up as Shay wrapped the vest around his torso. "Are you ready to work, Dex?" He barked a response, and the interaction put a smile on my face.

The duty belt was her final attachment, and I'll admit the full ensemble was impressive. I never had a thing for a woman in uniform until this one walked back into my life. "I'm seven-to-three again today. Are we forging tonight?" She fished her ponytail through the back of her hat, tugging it into place

"You're hooked. I knew you'd love it." I kissed her before she walked down the stairs and leaned against the doorframe, watching her go. "Have a good day at work, honey."

"You too, dear."

"Nope, nope, we can't do that. It sounds so domestic."

She waved a dismissive hand. "It doesn't have to be."

I blew her a last kiss. "See you later."

"If you go back to bed, I'm going to be very jealous."

"Sorry, but I'm definitely going back to bed. You keep ridiculous hours."

She closed the door, and I heard the key turn the lock back into place. I hated the emptiness of my apartment without them. I lingered over the notes on the kitchen table before climbing back into bed. My hand clenched her pillow, and I could still smell the scent of her in the room. I stared up at the ceiling, but I didn't get to sleep at all.

My phone vibrated on the bedside table. "Wildwood Blackstone," I answered.

"Hey, Wildwood, it's Bill Bailey out at the Bailey farm. We've got a small problem out here. You got time this morning to help us with a hitch?"

"I've got plenty of time this morning." I ran my hand through my hair. "Give me half an hour, and I'll be there. Your repair is out on the farm, right?"

"Yep. Get on South, and keep going 'til you can't. We're sitting in the ditch."

Bill Bailey had been my first paying job in Bannock, and I was glad to get this second call. A welding distraction was exactly what I needed. It took me a few minutes to throw my gear into the back of my little truck. Giving up the Volkswagen Bug was a hard decision, but it was time to own something more convenient. The drive was beautiful, and twenty minutes later, I was out on a call, doing trailer repairs in a ditch on the side of a road. There was something very satisfying about a truck full of guys watching me work.

I leaned down, trying to make a quick assessment of the damage as the owner approached. "Hey, Bill." I shook his hand.

"Hello again, Wildwood. I tried to call you and let you know we had it all jacked up."

I patted my pockets, feeling around for my cell phone. "I must have set my phone down in the shop when I was loading the truck. Let me just take a look."

He hovered over my shoulder. "What do you think?"

"I think your guys need to take it easy in the ditches."

He laughed. "We've had about an hour to talk about that while we were waiting for you. Damn kids."

"This shouldn't take me too long. Just ask the guys to watch traffic." That was the end of the conversation. I threw a bright orange cone behind my truck and got to work. The repair was simple for me. I did a quick cutaway of the break and cleaned the surface with an angle grinder.

I set up the welder, but I was still thinking about last night. Why did I just burst into the room? Why didn't I wait? Why did I have to react the way that I did? Watching her fall apart was impossible to forget, but maybe this was a leap forward to helping Shay find safety with me. It was too soon to really know. I snugged the welding helmet on my head, flipped it over my face, and concentrated on the work in front of me.

The job took most of the morning and was ultimately the perfect distraction. "I'll send you an invoice when I get back to the shop," I explained.

"I'll take it out of their wages." He hitched his thumb toward the farm boys waiting in the truck. "Thanks again, Wildwood."

"Happy to help." I loaded my gear, flipped that cone into the bed of the truck, and drove back to the shop. I was unloading my gear when I noticed my cell phone ringing on the table. Her number displayed, and I was excited to hear the voice on the other end. "Hello, Shay."

"Hello."

"I was just getting home. Are you still planning to come after work?" There was silence on the other end. "Shay?"

"Wil, can you meet me over at Slammed?"

The tone in her voice was serious, and it scared me. "Are you okay?"

"Yes, I'm fine. Just meet me at Slammed. Now, please."

I looked at the display, noticing four missed calls from her. I threw my tools into the shop and was at the bar in less than five minutes. Shay's squad car was parked out front, but neither she nor Dexter was anywhere in sight. I asked one of the officers at the scene. He squeezed the radio on his shoulder, and a few seconds later, she met me at the door. "Alex, will you add Wildwood Blackstone to the list, please."

"I got her, Shay."

"Thanks, man." She led me inside the bar. It was empty except for the police presence and retired officer Regina Benton.

I had no idea why I was there. I reached for her shoulder. "Will you tell me what's going on?" I grabbed her wrist when I noticed the stain on her arm. "What the hell is that?"

She looked down at her sleeve. "Don't worry. It's not mine."

"That's not very comforting," I said, surveying the damage to the bar. The door to Benton's small office was leaning against the wall. I guessed it was kicked off the hinges. I felt the crumble of glass beneath my feet, swishing the frothy pools of beer around them. Two legs of a chair rested on the table as we walked through. Benton sat on the edge of the cushioned bench, her head tilted back against the worn vinyl. Her arm was wrapped in gauze, but I could see the stain of blood seeping through. I resisted reaching out to touch her as I asked, "What the hell happened?"

"Sit down, Wildwood, and we can fill you in." I followed her directions and listened as they shared the details from the night before.

"I did what I've been doing for the last two years. I locked the front door. I cleared the bar. I turned the last few chairs up so I could mop the corner." She pointed to the back of the bar. "I shouldn't be so damn predictable. Taking the garbage out to the dumpster is the last thing I do. I'm such an idiot." She rubbed the back of her head. "Someone followed me when I came in. I wasn't paying attention."

Shay was writing notes in a small pad. She paused and pointed her pen at Benton but looked at me. "She didn't call the station until a few hours ago."

I leaned in to get a closer look at the arm. "Why aren't you at the hospital?"

Shay interrupted to answer. "She refused to go, even though she hit her head and she can't remember how long she was out."

Benton was getting upset with Shay. "Will you just back off and let me make decisions for myself?" She pushed away from the table and lost her balance trying to stand on unsteady feet.

"This is such bullshit." Shay squeezed the mic on her shoulder, at the same time trying to balance her friend. "Pierce to base."

Her radio burst with static. "Go for Pierce."

"Can we get a bus back over to Slammed?"

"I'm not getting in an ambulance, Shay," Benton yelled.

"Yes, you are, even if I have to cuff you to the damn stretcher."

I helped Benton back to the chair. "Does anyone want to tell me why I'm here?"

"According to Benton, you were the last person in the bar."

I looked around the room for the K-9 unit. "I was, I guess. Dexter and I went for a walk and ended up here." I watched the dog sniffing the outside edge of the room.

"Did you notice anything out of the ordinary?" Shay was running through obvious questions.

My answer was the same. "I was distracted. I didn't really notice anything." I pointed to the only other witness. "Dex was with me. I think he would have alerted me if we were in danger."

Shay nodded. "He's got a great nose for fear."

The ambulance arrived again. This time, Shay and I convinced Benton to go for an exam. She grumbled on her way out the door, but it was the right decision. I watched Shay. She was solid and unwavering, but I worried about what came after the investigation was over. I didn't ask questions until we were outside and away from her coworkers. "How are you doing?"

"I'm good." I could see that she wasn't, and I was beginning to understand what it took for her to do this job. "Dexter," she yelled for her partner.

"Will you still be off at three?"

She looked down at her watch. "I'm going to follow them to the hospital, and I'll be over when I'm finished." She walked around to the trunk of her car. "I need you to take these papers to the carriage house. Go through them, and tell me what you find."

"What am I looking for?"

She shrugged. "To be honest, I'm not sure. I'm hoping you'll know when you see it."

I lifted the box from the back of her squad. "What's in here? It feels like a box of rocks."

She slammed the trunk. "Those are Benton's unofficial papers —her private research and notes." She opened the back door, and Dexter jumped in. "She said they were scattered all over the office. She'd packed it up before we got there. I don't know what's going on, but Benton boxed up all of her demon research before calling me." She tugged at her vest, pulling it away from her side. "I don't know why Benton isn't telling me everything."

I leaned in to kiss her cheek. "I'll be in the apartment. Come when you can." She was already inside her car, radioing her location and intended destination. I dropped the box and grabbed the frame around the car window. "Are you okay?"

She nodded. "It's too close. It's just too close."

I didn't get a chance to ask more questions, but I knew that seeing Benton's injuries was hard on her heart. She was halfway down the street when I decided watching her go was never going to be easy.

CHAPTER XI

Scars

I stared at the empty box, cursing the papers and notebooks spread out on my table, realizing that I was better with my hands than my head. I don't like reading, and I have terrible retention of facts, but I'll show up to fix just about anything. This pile of documents and data was overwhelming, and the best I could do was sort through and organize them to make it easier for Shay.

Benton had a detailed list of every demon she'd encountered. I read the short summary she wrote when she recovered the material from the mass fairy grave. She seemed to be the keeper of secrets, and that fascinated me. "We really do need to talk, Ms. Benton."

I sat back in my chair, waiting for Shay. There wasn't much left to do, and as the time ticked away, I thumbed through more material. Benton had a strange method of documenting her work, leaving huge blank spaces between notations and pages. When I found references to our blacksmithed creatures, I added them to my own diary. I hoped my efforts would unravel a reason behind the attack.

I was asleep in my chair when Dexter flopped his paws in my lap. "Hi, Dex." If he was a little faster, I might not have been caught in my prone position.

Shay was a fiery, powerful woman, beautiful inside and out, but tonight, she looked wrecked. Her left hand clenched the bloodied ball of her uniform shirt. Her naked arms, revealing the scars of her past, were an immediate sign of exhaustion. "How are you?"

She had a duffle over her shoulder that dropped to the floor. "I'm finished with this day." I guessed the bag held her duty belt and a change of clothes.

"What can I do?" I asked.

She was quiet. This part of our relationship was new, and although I thought I understood how she felt with regard to her job, the reality of Benton's assault complicated everything. I heard the velcro tear away from her vest, and she dropped it on the floor. "I just want to sleep." She dragged her duffle to the bathroom, and before I could even ask I heard the shower running. This was her; she was showing me the complexities of her job. Bad days didn't stay out on the street. They came home. If I was going to love her, be with her, I was responsible for taking care of the softer side of Shay.

Dexter was looking at me. He was still wearing his vest. I took it off, and he found a cozy spot in the corner of the room. "You hungry, buddy?" I scooped some food into his dish and filled his bowl with water. I had a thousand questions about what happened today, but they all had to wait. She needed me. I put a glass of water beside the bed and changed into sweatpants. The air in the apartment was cool as I waited.

She was toweling her hair when she came into the room. Her T-shirt was long, hanging midway to her thigh. "Your water gets so hot. It was perfect." The skin of her arms was bright pink, highlighting all of the scars. She was a walking example of courage.

"Yep. Nothing like a hot shower."

The towel came off, and I could see the dark shadows of exhaustion under her eyes. "Come to bed, Shay."

She stood there, holding the damp towel, her red hair blackened from the moisture of the shower. "I'm not good at this." She took the towel back to the bathroom and turned out the lights. She was avoiding me—us. She turned to leave. "Dexter needs . . ."

"I took care of Dex." I patted the empty space beside me. "Just come to bed."

She stopped in the doorway, grabbing the frame for support, her back to me. "I'm going to disappoint you."

I threw the covers aside and stepped in behind her. "We aren't going to do anything right now but sleep."

"I'm not going to . . ." She turned to look at me. "I was going to go to my house tonight, but I didn't want to sleep alone."

"I would be on your front porch right now, beating down the damn door, if you'd done that."

"I know." She pulled her hair away from her face. "I've never had anyone for this."

"For this what?" I asked.

"For the after."

She was breaking my heart. "I'm here. You don't have to do this by yourself."

"I don't want to. Not anymore."

"Then you don't have to." I squeezed her hands and led her across the room to the bed. She climbed in on my side and pressed herself against me as I slid behind her.

"I'm not okay, Wil."

"I know." I held her long after my shoulder lost feeling and my arm fell asleep. She rolled across my body, and a few minutes later, I rested.

CHAPTER XII

Accord

It was slightly annoying that Shay was awake long before me. When I heard Dexter in the kitchen, I knew she wasn't very far away. I could smell the coffee, and in an instant, my feet were on the floor. I didn't stop to brush my teeth or to comb my hair. I could already tell it was going to be a four-cup morning. Shay looked good standing at my kitchen table. Her smile was the first thing I wanted to see after every sunrise. "Hi, you."

She looked up from the notebook. "Hello, my sleeping beauty."

I laughed, giving Dexter a pat as I walked to Shay. "I'm hardly a princess, but I do feel like I slept for a week."

"I do too." She handed me a cup for my coffee. "I just made it."

"Have you been up long enough to drink an entire pot?"

She shook her head. "I need a kiss before you begin the interrogation."

I complied. She felt wonderful in my arms as I relaxed against her body. "I could get used to this."

"I could too," she said.

"How long have you been going through all of the notes?"

She sat down in front of the organized piles. "I was up with my alarm. It's a hard habit to break."

I leaned against the kitchen counter. "I can see that's going to be an adjustment for me."

I watched her look through my notes and the little folders I'd sorted. "You made a great start with this," she said. "Most of the records are confirmation of the things we already knew, but I don't see any documentation on the runic incantations that we uncovered in the workshop."

"Her notes are so complex, and I don't understand the organization."

"There are a lot of blanks to fill in. That's for sure." Shay was flipping back and forth between the pages, focusing on her research. "Why did she leave all this empty space between?" She was distracted, and that was okay, but one question was hanging heavy on my conscience.

"Did my visit cause the attack?"

She looked up at me. "No, sweetheart."

"Are you sure?"

"I spent the entire afternoon with Benton. Gosh, she was so damn pissed. She kept saying that she didn't need a babysitter." Shay was smiling as she remembered. "I told her to stop being a baby and I would leave."

"How did that go over?"

"It didn't really." She summarized. "She couldn't describe the attacker, which made me wonder about the blow to her head.

The assailant was close to Benton's height, but she couldn't describe the weapon that slashed her arm. Everything that Benton remembers just leads to more questions. What I know for certain is that someone was looking for the bones of our demons. Benton and I talked, and we think that you and I should do the final forging just to make sure that the conversions are complete."

"Am I in danger here?" I motioned to emphasize the space of the carriage house.

She nodded. "I think that taking precautions would be a good idea."

I wandered through the second-story apartment. "This is the least secure building in the city of Bannock." I looked out at the emptiness of the glass-framed greenhouse, the dirt-filled buckets, and trays sprouting unidentified greenery.

"Yes, we discussed that too."

"I'm guessing our friend doesn't have any long-term injuries from the attack. She seemed pretty chatty."

"Oh, she has a concussion, two staples in her head, and they gave her arm eleven stitches." I was surprised by her flippant explanation.

"Is she still in the hospital?"

"She is. They wanted to watch her overnight. The tremors were sporadic, and the doctor was nervous."

"How are you doing with all of this?"

She stopped to take a breath and consider her words. "I'm worried about her and the reason for the attack, but mostly I'm worried about what it means for you."

"What you're trying to tell me is that I am in danger." I sat in the chair beside her.

She closed her eyes, taking a deep breath before answering. "You might be, and not just from demons."

"What are we going to do?"

"I considered a security setup, but the more I look at the building, the more I think we should do a protection glamour to keep the threats away."

"A magick alarm system?" I asked with a little too much excitement.

"Something like that, yes."

I didn't even try to hide my enthusiasm about watching her do magick again. "What do we need to do?"

"*We* need to take a walk to the house and grab a few things, and then *we'll* come back and take care of this building."

"You're going to let me help?"

"Every step of the way."

Her hand felt right in my own as we walked together to her house. We gave Dexter a chance to run around Shay's backyard before packing up books and supplies in the cart. This was becoming a regular occurrence, and I wondered how long it would be before the U-Haul was at my door.

Her laundry was piled in the corner. "Do you need to wash clothes or any of your work gear?"

"I dry-clean my shirts. Uniforms are issued by the department. That reminds me, I should order a new shirt."

"That freaked me out yesterday," I confessed.

"Yes, I know it did. I should have warned you, but we were ordered to withhold information until we had some answers."

"It brings up a lot of things that we need to talk about," I said.

"I'm pretty sure that I've been thinking about some of the same things," she replied, handing me books from the shelves and containers from the cabinet.

"I have to ask you a question that might be jumping ahead, but I need to know."

She stopped, standing with the cart of magic tools between us. "What do you need to know?"

"You realize that I love you and that I want to be with you, but having two homes is very hard."

She pointed to the collection of tools in front of her. "I know it is." She closed the cover on the cart and dropped her duffle on top. "Every time I pack a bag to stay with you, I wish you'd do the same for me, but here."

I pulled the cart to the front door. "You think this would be a better place to live?" I asked.

"I know it is for me."

It was clear that the two of us would need to discuss the pros and cons of apartment and home life. Even unfinished, my space was perfect. I was beginning to see that she felt the same way about her own.

"Dexter has a yard here," she explained. "The fence gives him room to roam and dirt to dig in."

"Your dog never digs in the dirt."

She smiled. "Maybe not, but that doesn't matter; he likes the freedom." She pointed to the beautiful German shepherd laying on the back porch.

"He looks like that most of the time."

She put her arm around my shoulder. "This house protects us. It protects me. I'm just not ready to let it go."

I was curious about her comment. "How does it protect you?"

"Dex," she called the dog. "Everything we are about to do at the carriage house, I've already done here."

"What does that mean?"

"Let's go back over, and I'll show you. It'll be easier with visuals." She clipped the lead to Dexter's collar, and we dragged the tool kit across town to the carriage house. All of our notes were spread out on the table upstairs, and Shay spent more than an hour matching her magick to fit the space of my building.

The corner of the kitchen was becoming an apothecary, and the small bookcase I'd built into the wall was the unofficial second library. I watched her open books and make notes on a loose piece of paper. "Tell me what you're doing."

"This book." She put her thumb on the page and flipped the cover so I could see it. "I use this for all of my practical magick."

"Is that really a thing?" The cover read *Practical Magick for the Practical Witch*. I was intrigued. "Who would write a book like that?"

"Regular practitioners. People who've had success with magick and want to help the rest of us who don't have time to mess with trial and error."

"Error?"

She was tearing a pile of herbs into a small container. "Sometimes you just have to wait and see if it works. Not this one though. I've used it on my home, and it keeps everything unwanted out."

"Does that include Andrea Peters?"

She stopped shredding the herbs and looked up at me. "I promise you have no reason to worry about Andrea."

"Are you sure? It felt like there was more than professional discord between you."

"We went out on a date . . . twice." She wrote a few words on her paper. "I knew after the first date that she wasn't my type. There isn't a kind or considerate bone in her body."

I was a little confused. "Why did you say yes to the second date?"

"That was Benton's fault. She set it up, not knowing about the first one."

"I'm guessing there are some hard feelings."

"Not from my side of things, but yes, Andrea Peters can hold a grudge."

"Did you kiss her?"

Shay looked at me. "Would it bother you if I did?"

I tried to play it cool, but she could see that I was bothered. "Maybe. I didn't like her before, so I certainly won't like her now."

"There was no kissing. I promise." Shay opened another book; this one was not about herbs, but focused on gemstones and crystals.

"That's good because I was going to have to question your taste in women."

"Maybe I should be asking you about all of your kisses." She dipped her fingers in the bottle of water and sprinkled it over the bowl. She added a few words to her notes.

"Ask away. I'm an open book." I started with the easiest. "There have been a few, short-term for the most part. I've dated two men. They were nice enough, but they fizzled out because I wanted to blacksmith more than anything. I've also dated a few women, but . . ."

She set down her pencil and walked next to where I was standing. "But?"

"They didn't make me feel the way I do when I'm with you."

"You are quite the sweet talker."

I shook my head at her comment. "I'm really not. I've just always wondered—dreamed, really—and then you were there. You do leave an impression."

She put her hand on the back of my neck and pulled me in for a kiss. "I know exactly how you feel. I think I would have wondered about you forever." I held tight to her forearms as she pressed her lips to mine. My mouth opened to hers, wanting more, desperate to connect like never before. I was dizzy, short of breath. She leaned back, looking into my eyes.

"Whoa." It was the only sound I could make. She knew exactly how to turn me inside out, and I was gone. "I guess we don't have to wonder anymore . . . ever."

"I want to touch you." My heart was racing. The only dream I'd ever wanted was happening in front of me, and I had to pinch myself to make certain it was real. My fingers moved to the button of my shirt, but she stopped me. "We have to do the ritual first." She held our hands over my heart. "When we're done, all of your senses will be heightened. It'll be like nothing you've ever experienced."

"So it'll be a day of firsts." I kissed her again before taking a step back. I watched her return to the table and sort through all of the tools she'd brought to the apartment.

"You ready to be part of your first protection incantation?"

"I'm not sure, but if you're leading, I'm always willing to follow."

"Everything has a purpose. If you don't understand, it's okay to ask." I nodded as she placed tools into the cart, and we carried it to the center of the workshop. She assembled the altar, placing candles in the north and south directions of the permanent circle on the floor. I couldn't stop myself from asking questions, and as crazy as I thought they might be, Shay was patient and loving with her answers. "Are we going to let the gatekeeper out of here?"

"No, we are not." She handed the notes to me. "These are the translated runes on the wall behind you. Light the wick of the demon candleholder."

"Are you serious?"

She nodded. "Use the Dagger of Doom, just like the last time."

I rolled my eyes at her use of the name, but I obeyed. I sparked the knife against the handle, and the blue flame flickered. "I'll never get over this."

She smiled at me. "I have to admit, it's pretty damn cool." She waved me closer. "Use the blue flame to light the charcoal in the censer, and then we'll walk the circle."

I did everything she asked. "Take this." It was the jar of white powder she was always shaking around the circle.

"What is it?"

"It's salt," she answered.

"I'm pretty sure I know why you use salt, but will you explain it to me?"

"Salt represents the earth element." She drew a line with a huge piece of white chalk. "It's extremely important for purification." She held the jar in my hand and shook the container over the ring she'd drawn on the concrete floor. "Just follow my line all the way around, and repeat after me."

She let go and stepped in the center, holding her paper. She looked up as if speaking to the universe. "This is the salt from the earth. Bless this circle. Consecrate this ring in the name of the goddess."

I said every single word exactly as she did, and when I was done drawing the ring of salt, Shay sat down in the center. She held two black candles, running each through the oils she'd poured into the palm of her hand. She handed them to me. "Light these candles with the blue flame, and set them in front of me and behind me." She sprinkled the herbs she'd torn on top of the censer charcoal. The smoke billowed up in a thick cloud.

I twisted the thick wax tapers into the salt after adjusting their position. The scent of pine trees filled the air. The flames burned bright white. Her voice broke the silence. "Mother Goddess, I invoke your spirit and wisdom. With smoke and fire, I bless this circle." She stood, unfolded the dark robe by her side, and cinched it around her neck. She looked beautiful, holding the paper, invoking goddesses and gods I never knew existed.

She sat down in the center and placed the athame in front of her. She waved for me to come. Sitting face to face, we held hands. "Everything I say, repeat it." She smiled at me, adding, "In English this time."

Her hands were warm, and I could feel the transfer of light energy the moment we touched. I heard the sounds of the Earth so much like when we were children, but this time, she was leading me to an even brighter place.

"Coming together with a common purpose in light, in love, unite goodness for protection. Maiden, Mother, Crone, Sunlight, Twilight, Moonlight, on this side of shadow and beyond, safety lies with me, around me." She placed her hand over her heart. "This is the shield of protection." We chanted continuously until the black tapers burned to the floor. I'd lost track of the world aside from the voice in front of me and the heat where our bodies still touched. After almost an hour, the blue flame was the only light in the room. The runes on the wall in front of Shay beamed, and she scratched them on the floor with the chalk. I wondered if she knew what it meant, but I wasn't breaking the focus of our circle.

She squeezed my hands. "Close your eyes." She stood up and moved to sit behind me. I felt her arms come around my hips to rest in my lap. "Weave your fingers into mine." The whisper of her voice in my ear was like the song of an angel. In that moment, I would have done anything she asked. I could feel my heart pounding and wondered if every point where her body was touching me revealed my excitement. "Breathe, my love." I wasn't holding my breath, but I knew what she was saying. Her right hand came up over my heart. "I am the light. She is the light. We are the light." Her left hand reached out to the side. "Receive protection, give protection, be protection." I started to repeat her words. "Shh . . . This is my gift to you."

I can't remember ever feeling so invigorated or alive. Our bodies, together in the purest form of loving kindness, filled every broken part I'd ever burdened to carry. If I called it love as a breathing being, it wouldn't come close to defining what was happening between us. I relaxed into her arms, feeling her laugh against me. She whispered again, "By the goddess, you are so completely perfect."

I didn't know how long we sat until her hands moved against my skin. "Tell me what you feel right in this moment."

"Safe. I feel safe." I had no idea my voice could sound so breathy. The magick that was Shay had that effect on me.

Her finger pushed across the back of my neck, sliding my hair away to reveal the tender skin. The first touch of her lips was like a feather, sending tiny pebbled bumps over my flesh. "You're always going to be safe with me, Wildwood." She tugged at the shirt clinging to my shoulder. Everywhere her lips kissed, fire moved through me. When she said our senses would heighten, I wasn't prepared for how ferociously I would desire her touch.

I turned against her body. "Did you put a spell on me, Shay Pierce?" I kissed her before she could answer. My hands were in her hair, tugging it from the tangled bun.

"Wildwood." My name coming from her lips was all I wanted. "I think you put a spell on me long before I ever knew what magick was."

"Unless you tell me to stop, I want to make love to you."

"I've never wanted anything more in my entire life."

Her words were breathy, and I was aware of everything in the room. "Can we get up now?"

"You might need to help me," she said with a chuckle.

I stood first, suddenly aware of what she meant. The magick was exhausting, disorienting, and invigorating all at the same time. I held a hand to her and led us up the stairs to our room. I unclipped the cloak from her shoulders, letting it fall to the floor. "I'm going to touch you. Can I?"

I could see a whirlwind of emotions in her eyes. "Yes."

I pinched the top button of her shirt. I separated each, lingering over them one at a time. I wanted her to stop me if that was her choice, but she didn't. The front of her blouse fell apart, and I could see the skin of her abs and the swell of her breasts. "No bra?"

"Only in uniform."

I'd never seen her completely naked, but I'd dreamt about it a thousand times. I pushed the collar over her shoulders, and the fabric fell in a pile on the floor. My hand trailed across her shoulder and rested at the nape of her neck. I touched her chin and pulled her in for a slow, deliberate kiss. I wanted to remember everything about this day.

My hands came around her back but hesitated when I touched a scar on her torso. I felt her sharp intake of air and stopped. "Are you okay?" She nodded, but I wasn't convinced. "Shay?"

"No one has ever touched me." She looked down at her body. "Them."

I knew what she was saying, but I wanted her to share everything she was feeling. "Tell me, love. I'm not afraid."

"I am." Her eyes closed, and when they opened again, the tears forming multiplied the intensity of the green.

"Maybe we should wait? Slow down?" Shay shook her head, moving my hand against her stomach. My fingertips traced the dimpled edges of the three wounds just below the line where her bra would fit. "Tell me?"

I could see the emotions in her eyes: embarrassment, sadness, and most of all—fear. Tumbling back in time, to this dark memory was a doorway she could never close again. "I'm not sure how, and I want you to be with me."

"Do you think I won't want to because I know?"

She didn't say a word. She just tipped her head, and my heart was breaking all over again. "I'm going to love you for the rest of my life, Shay, but if I'm going to touch you, I need to understand when to stop."

She stepped away, and the retelling came in tiny bursts. "I know you've seen my arms, my hands." She held them out for me. I confirmed this with a silent nod. "The first puncture was to my back." She took a deep breath. "It was also the deepest. The hospital intake picture shows dark bruising from the hilt of her knife." She tried to reach around, but it was beyond the tips of her fingers. "I'd read a book that said if you prostrate on your stomach that your spell will be more powerful. That's what I was doing. The knife penetrated my lung, which made it hard to yell for help."

I turned her around so I could see the wound. My caress began at the nape of her neck and paused over the fading scar. I could feel her ribs in my hand as I pulled our bodies together. My kiss was meant to take away her pain, and her quiet gasp was all the encouragement I needed. She turned to show me the wounds on her chest.

"I rolled over—I guess by instinct because I wasn't quite aware—and she hit me here"—Shay touched each scar—"here, and here."

These were the permanent marks, the complex remnants of trauma that brought tears to my own eyes. "Oh, my love." She leaned away, trying to put distance between us. "Do you want me to stop?" I asked.

Her head shake moved the grief from her eyes. "You're so gentle. I don't want you to stop." She stood between my legs, and I held her, focusing on the tears as my hand reached up to touch her.

She stopped my fingers inches away from her skin. "Please don't let this ruin us." I kissed the scar on the back of her right hand and then her left. I held them to the side so I could see her bare abdomen.

"These are never going to come between us, not for one more single moment." I kissed each scar with a featherlight touch of my lips. I could feel her heart racing—or maybe it was my own—as I pulled away. "Your scars are so damn beautiful." She closed her eyes, arching against me as I ran a finger across each point my kisses touched. "So beautiful."

I worshipped her body like I'd never been with another. Her breathing was labored as I felt her excitement build. I touched the scar under her arm. "This one is . . .?"

She rubbed it with her own fingers. "The doctors had to put in a chest tube. I was awake for that, and it hurt like hell." I rotated her hips and pressed a kiss over the tented skin. The walls that protected Shay crumbled with every touch until she surrendered to love, deciding to let me in.

She tugged at the collar of my shirt. "Wildwood, you're wearing an awful lot of clothes." Her knees came up along my thighs as she climbed across my lap.

I fell back on the bed, pulling her down on top of me. Her palms planted alongside my head, and her hair draped the side of her face. My heart beat like a thundering drum as the most beautiful bright green eyes hovered above me. I was certain the wanting was mutual as I sat up to meet her and kissed her lips, opening my mouth to her own. I pulled my shirt over my head, and seconds later, she was beneath me, skin to skin. My hand came up to touch her breast, and I knew I would never be the same.

Her fingers squeezed my hips, and even though I was nowhere near her level of fitness, I was completely comfortable as she explored my body. Shay's fingertips trailed between my breasts, and she pressed her hand to my heart. "I love you, Wildwood."

My hips moved as my leg slipped between her own. I vowed to adore her forever as her back arched up with every motion. I wasn't sure I could contain the fire in my soul as our bodies came together. I didn't want to stop. I never wanted to let her go. "I love you too."

CHAPTER XIII

Veracity

She was asleep in my arms at four o'clock in the afternoon. I was on my back, with her naked body pressing against my own. I couldn't see much of her, but I tried to memorize every muscle with my fingertips. Her hand covered the swell of my breast, and I wanted to stay locked together forever, but Shay never rested, not completely.

Her hand fell away from my chest, and I knew she was awake.

"Hello, you." My kiss got tangled in her hair.

Shay's arms draped over her head as she stretched away from me. Her satisfied smile was everything. "Hi."

My hand came up to meet hers and pressed our palms together. "How are you?" I rolled my fingertip across the scar. "Are you still okay with this, with what just happened between us?"

She closed her eyes. "I am more than okay. You were beautiful, amazing." She wrapped tighter against my body.

"I wanted us to be special."

"It was. You were." She tried to leave the bed.

I hugged her closer to me. "You can't get up. I don't want to get out of this

bed— maybe forever."

"In case you haven't noticed, it's four o'clock in the afternoon." She sat up. "We've got a few things to do before it gets dark."

"Can a few of them be me touching you and you touching me?"

She crawled across the top of the blanket. "Absolutely not in the way that you want. Not right now."

I grabbed her ankle. "Are you seriously going to climb over me, naked, and just get out of this bed?"

She kicked away from my grasp and rolled to the edge of the mattress. "I am. Because if I don't, your house will be haunted again."

Slumping over, I rejected every word coming from her mouth. "Is it so terrible if I want to bask in the afterglow of sex." Was it possible to be offended by the sound of my own whining voice?

She laughed at me as she walked to the bathroom. I could hear her trying to talk through the foam of her toothbrush. "It wasn't a one-night stand." I didn't respond to her mumbling. I heard her spit into the running water. "It wasn't, was it?" I refused to get out of the bed or answer her question until she came into the room. I wanted to see her body. I wanted her to come back to me. She returned, giving me half a glimpse as she lingered in the doorway. "Well, was it?"

I pretended not to hear her.

"Wildwood!" I made it obvious I was staring at her body. "Perv. Never mind, I can see the answer in that smirk on your face."

I jumped out of bed and grabbed her hand before she went back to the bathroom. "You would never be a one-time anything." I wiped the toothpaste from her lip.

Her kiss was a quick peck. "Good. Now get some clothes on. We have work to do."

I leaned against the frame of the door, watching her walk away. I pinched myself just to be certain that all of her was real.

Shay walked by, wearing clothes that I decided I would despise for the rest of the day. "You can work naked, but I'm not going to accomplish much if you do." She touched my cheek as she walked by. "Clothes get kisses."

I kicked into my pants and shoes. I picked up my shirt and pulled it over my messy head. A quick comb through with my fingers and I was out the door. "Clothes get kisses." I waved over the length of my body. "Bonus for shoes?"

She looked up from the piles of paper on the table. "Get over here."

I thought I was getting kissed, but she was more distracted by the notes. "Did you know that the class-one specimen is part of a spire?"

"Are we really going to do this?" I pushed the page out of her hand.

"You are adorable, and as much as I want to lay in bed with you for the rest of my life—and I really do—I need to know that you're safe."

"What could be safer than me in your arms?"

She thought about it for a second. "Finishing the protection and binding before you get to be safe in my arms."

"Fair enough compromise." I held her papers behind my back. "I have the clothes. I require the kisses."

She pinned me against the table. "I'll kiss you." It was the most chaste peck on the cheek. Her arms came around my body, and she snatched the pages from my hands.

"That was so wrong. Some kind of superhero you are."

"They always get the girl, don't they?"

"Not always." I moved to the opposite side of the table.

She didn't look up from the work in front of her. "Reel it in, Blackstone. We've got work to do." She was reading the documents as she walked to the stairs. "Are you planning to help me?"

What a dumb, damn question. Of course I was going to help her. I'd already promised to follow her anywhere. We had a job to finish. When my feet hit the bottom step, I stopped to watch her lay out the tools on the floor. "I see the demon flame is still going."

She laughed. "The whole thing is amazing to me. I'm guessing it's the ability of this demon to lead or guide." She set the candle on the floor in front of the wall. She added the runes to her notes.

"Isn't that what the gatekeeper is too?"

"He's class-two but has different elements in his transformation. The punch daggers are proof of that."

"What do you think it is? What's the constant?"

She held up her sketch. "I'm guessing that it's you."

I saw the blue light of the candle shining in front of the circle on the wall. It was my maker's mark drawn a hundred years before I'd ever stepped inside the building. "So now what?"

"I think it's time for your favorite thing."

"Making love to my girlfriend?"

She threw the pages at me. "Not that. Damn, I really have created a monster."

"Only in the most loving and consensual way."

"Yes."

I picked up everything she'd thrown in my direction and laid it out in front of her. "Solve the riddle, superhero."

"That's my plan if you can keep your damn pants on."

I walked away. "I'm going to take Dexter for a walk with my damn pants on. You want to come with us?"

A dismissive wave was her only response. I knew that the rest of the afternoon would involve books, blue candlelight, and lots of pencils, all while keeping our clothes on. I wasn't thrilled about any of them. The dog was excited to see me and came when I called him from the bottom stair. I didn't have a destination in mind when we left, but we wandered our way to Shay's porch and that orange door. There was no mail in her mailbox when I checked. I tightened my grip on the leash moments before Dexter pulled me down the steps. We walked by the bar, where I stopped to peek in the window. Dex was looking for his friend, or maybe he remembered that steak. I wondered when Benton would come home.

Dexter liked to run, and I did not, but I hoped that, in time, we could balance each other on these evening walks. When we returned to the carriage house, Shay was standing in the workshop, staring at the candle flame in the corner opposite the giant circle. Her hair was pulled back away from her face, and I stopped to admire the woman in front of me. Was it possible that she was finally my lover? It didn't seem real.

"You going to ogle me for the rest of the day?" She didn't turn around.

I had no idea what she was doing, or if my presence would interrupt her work. "I'm being careful."

She started to lay her drawings out along the wall. "It's always good to try new things."

"You're funny." I crossed my arms in defiance.

"I thought you knew that about me."

"I'm learning."

She leaned against the wall in the most inviting way. "You want to come over here and help me?"

She knew that I did. "What are we doing now?"

"Research. More research." She handed a notebook to me.

"Is this what our future holds?"

She stood behind me. "Yes, my love. It'll be a very big part." Her arms came around me. "But I promise there'll be so much more."

Thank you for reading book one of the Maker Series, the continuing story of Wildwood Blackstone, a lady blacksmith who finds adventure, demons, magick and love in the small ghost town of Bannock.

MARK OF THE MAKER (BOOK 1)

Wildwood Blackstone believed her dream of being a country blacksmith was coming true. When the town of Bannock hires her to restore their abandoned carriage house built in the 1800s, she can't wait to begin.

But there are more than ghosts in Bannock and shortly after her arrival she discovers this truth. When a childhood friend answers a call for help, Wildwood finds a part of her past that she longed to rediscover. Together they reveal Bannock's secret and uncover the Mark of the Maker.

THE MAGICK AND THE MAKER (BOOK 2)

Wildwood Blackstone longed for a life as a small-town blacksmith. She didn't imagine monsters or magick, and she never expected to fall in love with Shay.

Book two of the Maker Series finds the two women tangled together in the dark secrets buried deep in Bannock's small-town history. Is their commitment strong enough to carry them through? Who is the keeper of the Magick? When will Wildwood and Shay uncover the mystery behind the Mark of the Maker?

THE ORIGIN OF THE MAKER (BOOK 3)

Wildwood and her girlfriend Shay have uncovered Brigid's secret hidden deep in the earth.

Who is the stranger in the carriage house? How are they there? What do they know about the secret and the power it holds? Can Wildwood and Shay find the answers and keep fighting the monsters hunting them night and day? Find out in book three of the Maker Series. Origin of the Maker Coming in 2022.

THE LEGACY OF THE MAKER (BOOK 4)

In a secret world filled with magick, Wildwood Blackstone has encountered unbelievable mysteries. As the blacksmith in her new hometown, she's survived and endured the call to wield the hammer of the goddess Brigid, but to what end?

Celebrating a year with her girlfriend, Shay, the two continue their search for answers. What lived inside Andrea Peters? How did the entity survive for hundreds of years? Who controlled her all this time?

Their call to be The Magick and The Maker of Bannock comes with more questions than ever, but it might also come with answers to their past. Wildwood and Shay are drawn into endless realms, all of which lead to the Legacy of the Maker.

MORE ROMANCES

Rage Room Romance Series

CONNED (Book 1)

For Ella Eastman, firefighting is life. She's devoted her body to being the best, but everyone needs a break from reality once in a while. For Morgan Hail, art is life, but she has to make a living. Their lives collide when television fandoms intersect at The Blacktree Comic Palooza.

Morgan's captivating fanart leads to a heated misunderstanding, and a cosplay contest brings these two women together–though only one of them knows the truth. This unlikely pair heats up when their real-world lives collide, but what will happen to their budding romance when Ella reveals her secret identity? And can they find a way to make things work when Ella's job hits a little too close to home? Conned is a story of love, loss, new beginnings, and fandom.

DECONSTRUCTED (Book 2:)

After eight years, Ella Eastman has a plan to create the perfect marriage proposal for her partner, Morgan. Inspired by Morgan's to-be-read pile, Ella struggles to incorporate her favorite romance tropes while asking the big question. The ideas pile up, as do the failed attempts to create their once-in-a-lifetime memory. How do you give the perfect partner the perfect memory of a perfect proposal? For Ella, it all seems to come together quite imperfectly. Revisit the Rage Room Romance's chosen family as they unite for Operation Perfect Proposal.

The Alice and Violet Stories

YULE BE HOME FOR SOLSTICE (Alice and Violet Book I)

Violet and Alice's December road trip is definitely a trial by transport as they set out to deliver the perfect Yule log for the Solstice celebration. This cross-state drive commemorates twenty years of sapphic bliss and three hundred thousand miles on their Subaru Outback named Bess. What happens between home and Aunt Eunice's house is a romantic comedy of errors. Sit back and enjoy this *Planes, Trains, and Automobiles*-style adventure to deliver the perfect Yule log for Winter Solstice.

DOUBLE DYNO

Prequel to Yule Be Home For Solstice (Alice and Violet Book II)

On a two-week hiking and climbing tour, Al Hadley guides a small team toward high adventure. With her best friends PB and Britt making up the Extreme Adventure Group, the goal is to build confidence and experience for each client. What they weren't counting on was Violet Crest and her amateur adventuring ways.

Weeks of planning and detailed maps can't tame Violet's curious nature. She's determined to make every moment count by capturing as many as possible through her camera lens, testing the boundaries and the patience of AEG's team leader, Al.

Dig into the story before the love story, in this slow burn, opposites attract, adventure and the prequel to *Yule Be Home for Solstice*.

Available now in print, eBook, and audiobook.

BEHIND THE EYES

Theirs was a love story for the ages: Rasabel, the captain of the guard, and Isolde, the woman of the territory. In a world of swords and arrows, love could not defend against a cruel curse. For years, they searched for an end.
When the alarm bells of Acadia ring, Rasabel goes home, but she is not welcome. Her path collides with Bylyn, a young thief on the run from the executioner's axe. Their lives are forever entangled.
Can Rasabel and Isolde find hope in the hands of a girl who will do anything to keep her freedom?

MORE FROM THE AUTHOR

DEAR KANE; WHAT I WISH WE WOULD HAVE SAID

Do the words that we say in front of our children build them up or tear them down? This short story explores the consequences of hatred and bigotry when it applies, unknowingly, to someone that you love. There's a time in every relationship when a parent must let go of the dreams they have for their child, so the child can chase what they dream to become.

IMMORTAL HUMAN TRUTH

Immortal Human Truth is a collection of poetry written by the author as she traveled to promote her first book Dear Kane; What I wish we would have said.

Each section explores experiences with love, injustice, loss and triumph of the spirit.

SHE BELIEVED SHE COULD

What can you do in a single day? Why haven't you done it yet? Jump out of your comfort zone and dive into life as you follow the author on her journey to achieve 365 new experiences in 365 days.

ABOUT THE AUTHOR

Sharon K Angelici, she/her, was born in the American Midwest, but her heart and soul belong to the mountains of Colorado.

She began writing as a child, using words to recover from trauma-induced depression. As a member of the LGBTQ+ community, she's an advocate for depression awareness and suicide prevention. In 2016 she published her first book dealing with both subjects, Dear Kane; what I wish we would have said.

Sharon is a full-time lover of life and all things Pagan and Magick. She's an artist and blacksmith, which inspired her to create her new Maker series. Book one Mark of the Maker released in 2020, and the second, The Magick and the Maker, to release in July of 2021.

Mark of the

Maker

Copyright 2020